Love *Lifted* Me

Love Inspired Series

VANESSA RICHARDSON

THE CERTAIN
ONES PUBLISHING, LLC

ISBN: 0692243011
ISBN-13: :978-0692243015

DEDICATION

To all the "Fight like a Girl" warriors and to the estimated 176 million women and young girls worldwide and those 8.5 million in North America endometriosis sisters. You are awesome!

ACKNOWLEDGMENTS

I want to acknowledge that without God all that I do would not be possible. I AM because of Him. Thank you, God! I want to thank my team who has supported me from day one. In spite of how crazy the goals are; you still chose to stick with me.

To my editor Keith at Unspoken Words. Thank you for help taking this book to a whole other level! You really got it! Your time and dedication was stellar and truly appreciated. Book cover designed by Tyora Moody. Photo by Artige' Tamaro Johnson photography, Charlie and Albordine Robinson.

To all the readers of The Certain Ones Magazine our listeners of The Certain Ones Blog Talk Radio --thank you! Your support gives me the strength to continue no matter how hard or lonely the roads traveled becomes.

Also by Vanessa Richardson

The Certain Ones: You're Not Forsaken. You're Chosen for

Purpose.

Love Found Me

www.VanessaRichardson.net

CONTENTS

Prologue

Victoria was in a battle, had been so ever since she could remember. She was battling to live or to die. Surely death was better than her harsh existence and that was what she'd been doing, existing. The land of the living proved too difficult - to painful.

The sound of birds chirping reminded her of the time. It was early morning and she had survived another night; survived to see another day. What others would hail as the gift of life, she labeled the grief of life. She would have to rustle up her next meal, a daunting task when not working. Sighing, she looked down at her slight frame, swiped at her stringy shoulder length tresses and rolled her eyes at what she saw.

Victoria looked like a prepubescent teenager and not a woman in her early twenties. Sometimes this had worked to her advantage; she had been able to slip through narrow gaps to escape danger, something that had occurred frequently.

"I don't need anyone." Her voice was soft, trembling. She swiped angrily at the tears falling suddenly from her eyes. She could feel the onset of a great burden, a flood threatening to unleash itself. Closing her eyes she counted steadily, inhaling and exhaling.

Minutes later, she felt she had regained control, although that one emotion she could never escape lingered. No matter how hard she tried to rid herself of it, it clung on stubbornly. Anger. She was angry at the world, life and people. "I am doing just fine on my own." Soft-spoken words that sounded louder but no less pitiful in her mind.

"An extra body would just slow me down." She stretched lazily, sighing as she ignored the creaking and cracking of her bones. "Nah, I am just fine on my own," she declared, half resolute, half-hearted.

She lived a nomadic life. Since the age of thirteen she had not been able to stay in one place for too long. Somehow "they" always found her. Always. Rolling on her side she became aware that she was crying, as cool fluid streaks rolled across her face. For years now all she'd seemed to do was cry. Truth be told, she had once thought that eventually a person would have to become all cried out. Seemingly hurt can cause a deep well that never runs dry. Now, she felt no need to stem the flow.

"Well, just you, boy. You're all I need." A slow smile touched her lips as she instinctively reached out to stroke Sabastien who pawed playfully at her face. He was a stray cat that she'd found and hastily named three days ago.

Sabastien lay still and she could see his gracefulness, beyond the mere visual physicality. The creature's short fur was a random mix of black and white. His face was disfigured with a pronounced scare juddering from ear to nose; the probable result of a vicious and sustained attack, she thought.

He had wide bulging green eyes that never blinked, and which she had to regularly moisten using a pipette. Not aesthetic beauty, then, but bestowed with a contented air, and no less eager to playfully chase critters or spend long periods in grooming.

"Hey, baby, how are you this morning?" She crooned gently. Sabastien leaned amenably against her hand, purring loudly as she softly stoked his back. He's hungry, she thought. "Yeah, yeah, I know the routine, Sabastien." Flinging a worn blanket away from her, she moved stiffly, sitting upright and standing briefly before turning to face the bed and crouching. Automatically, she began to say her prayers, asking for protection and guidance. Finishing, she stood, stretching wearily before making her reluctant way to the kitchen. The groans of the floor boards in response to each step, hinted at their weakness. The dilapidated building that housed her was on its last legs. She did not complain as it served its purpose and befitted the austere neighborhood, the nick name of which, "Hell's Bowel", required little interpretation.

There were no sounds of children laughing while at play. No neighborly greetings; morning or evening. People kept to themselves. The nature of the place engendered a survival of the fittest mentality. No one trusted anyone else and the need for social interaction appeared entirely absent. It was the perfect hideaway for her. She trusted and certainly needed no one.

Reaching the small kitchen, she grimaced. The floor was in desperate need of a scrub. Where once, white tiles has lightened, now squares stained beige with neglect and cracks like veins darkened. She was deprived of funds but not dismissive of sanitation. Opening the defected refrigerator she hastily scanned its barren interior.

Victoria knew what she'd find; but for some reason had half hoped that more food would magically have appeared. She sigh, disappointed, nothing had changed. The contents were as they had been the day before, a half cartoon of half spoilt 2 percent milk, two slices of cheese and five crackers.

Grabbing the items she made her way back to the bed come living room. Dropping to the floor, she placed the precious meager cargo down. She looked over at Sabastien; his peculiar eyes staring doubtfully back at her. "Like Jesus, I guess this will be our last supper, boy." Sabastien yawned loudly as if bored and licked one paw.

She arched one brow. "Well, thanks for lending me your ears. Good to know my words matter to you." She prayed over the meager meal, breaking three of five crackers into crumbs, scattering them in Sabastien's dish, adding milk and grinding the mixture with her hands. She sandwiched the cheese between the remaining crackers and ate silently. She chose to ignore the thin constant trickles that steamed from her eyes and ran down her face. Sabastien moved in close and rubbed his coat against her leg, as if to comfort her.

"There has to a better life than this." Suddenly, her heart lurched, painfully. It had done that a lot lately. She shrugged it off assuming that it would settle; as it had before but this time, the pain sharpened, spreading down her left arm. She gasped loudly, placing her thin hand hard against her chest. She was unprepared for such deep pain, it sent her sprawling and she collapsed onto her back.

Her agonizing cry sent Sabastien scurrying across the room. The scale of the distress was immense. Another wave had her gasping for breath, sending her flying off the bed; her head pressing hard against the unforgiving floor. Her stomach contracted, and swiftly repelled its meager contents. Victoria continued to retch, even though there was nothing else to bring up.

Somewhere deep inside she could hear herself screaming for help. The room seemed to shrink and her breathing escalated. Sabastien's loud meowing amplified her pain. He crossed cautiously to her spot and huddled by her side. She placed a hand on his soft furry body as if to derive some kind of comfort but in the midst of her agony she pressed too hard, causing the creature to screech in loud protest.

The cat's eyes appeared to bulge even more than was normal; an ugly yet endearing sight. The next wave of suffering unleashed itself upon her. The cat reacted to the cries of its mistress pain, rearing, hissing venomously and clawing its way free. One paw scratching at her left arm as it pulled away to flee.

Don't be afraid.

Victoria eyes widened with astonishment. Above the turmoil, she heard the voice, and had the situation not been so grave she would have laughed. Victoria rolled from side to side as if to displace the thing that was hurting her. She closed her eyes tight in an effort to force herself back to sleep, seeking desperately for a way out from under the crushing pain.

She felt a tingling sensation on her face, a sort of caress of comfort. She heard a faint sound from somewhere, seemed as if it was coming from within her head. There was a soft fuzzy feeling and then a tender whisper. Victoria was fighting to stay awake but realizing she was losing the battle.

Be at peace, child. You are not alone.

She gasped; it had become a struggle against the pull of darkness. When she was eventually able to open her eyes, she scanned the empty room. She had heard a voice. She was quite certain of it. Was she going mad?

No, you are not. Your need is for rest. This struggle is almost over for you, but your journey is just beginning.

She tried to talk, her mouth moving rapidly but nothing came out. She was exhausted, energy drained, she had succumbed to the pull of darkness and blessed peace.

Chapter 1

He threw the jab with as much force as he could muster. Sweat was pouring down his brows, the salty droplets stinging his eyes. Eric Miller was battling his early morning demons. After all this time his memories of that fateful night had not lessened. Over the years it seemed as if the recollections had intensified as he'd passed, from childhood to manhood. Nothing he had tried had stemmed the flow, and for some time now, he had given up trying; believing himself to be deserving of the restless nights he endured.

Because, he was too late to save her. Too late.

Eric thumped the punching bag hard again and again. This was his constant routine; sleep eluded him. Eric would go downstairs into his gym and box until near sunrise.

Hitting the bag one last time, he crossed over to the mini-refrigerator and pulled out a bottle of water. He gulped satisfyingly. Instinctively he knew the sun would soon be rising. He placed the empty bottle into the refuse basket and walked up the stairs into the spacious living room; his favorite place in the house. His home. It had taken three years to build the place to his satisfaction; to construct, not simply as a place to be, but to build as a refuge.

By rote he stood silently before the large paned glass, looking out over the expanse of water, across the lake which bordered the rear of the property. His SLR camera to hand, he watched as the sun ascended, and at the moment, snapped a couple of shots. Capturing another dawn, as he'd captured the dawning or each day ever since he could remember. He was never content to simply watch the sunrise or set. These events represented a feat of nature that was an unwelcome reminded that life was a gift, in spite of the hell it could sometimes erupt into.

With the Sun well and truly established, it was time to start his day. In the master bedroom he prepared for work. Cuffs and keys, he thought, as he adjusted his uniform and carried out a final check to ensure he had all the gear he needed. As a Detective in The Georgia Police Department, it never did to be forgetful, a principle of his. There were several cases, each at different stages, to keep a track of. In particular, there was the NWO case that sat forefront in his mind.

A group of religious fanatics who appeared prepared to do anything, including kill, in order to assert their message. The New World Order, indeed. Eric took a deep breath and exhaled with deliberation. Through this act, he could feel the demons releasing their grip, the faint residue of their visit leaving him feeling empty, alone.

He was not one to be deceived by his emotions. He had a small group of friends and family who he knew loved him without condition. The twins, Bryan and Mike Montgomery, were his best friends. His brothers, although not by blood. Their parents, who he lovingly called Pops and Mom, had legally adopted both; him and his twin sister, Erica. That was after their mother had been brutally murdered.

He had been the seven year old witness of an event that had gone on to take his father away psychologically. A strong man, from what he could recall, who in the wake of such tragedy, had become a hollow shell to the extent that they could hardly remember their real father, now. The day of infamy, as he'd come to regard it bitterly, had stolen both their parents from them.

Pops and Mom Montgomery, close friends of their parents, had gone into action immediately, seeking full custody. However, in the interim the siblings had been sent to stay with a distant aunt on their Father's side. Aunt Marisol. She was evil in every step she took and while he'd suffered at her wicked hands, it was Erica who had borne the brunt of her envy. Aunt Marisol would force Erica to wear long dark and ill-fitted clothing. Erica's hair was always pulled back into a severe bun as was ordered by Aunt Marisol.

When the Erica and Eric spoke to her; they had to refer to her as "your Majesty." It was the verbal attacks that took the longest time to heal. Those were the longest three months of their lives but in the end, God had answered their prayers. As Pops and Mom would often recite, 'only He can answer prayers, so pray,' and it had always seemed evidently true, as they had found sanctuary and love in safe hands.

As he made ready to for work his cell chimed out a familiar tone. It was his twin, Erica. She was the only one who knew about his daily battle for sanity and she called religiously, to check up on him. He was older by 2 minutes, to hear her tell it, it seemed like two years. Eric took his job as big brother seriously, Erica was his heart.

"Morning, baby girl," Eric greeted affectionately.

"Good morning, big brother." Erica sang out.

Eric detected the sound of background traffic at Erica's end of the line; he looked at the clock - 6:30 AM.

"I wanted to run the details by you." By details she meant her work schedule. Erica planned her life to a T and she was never without one of her many planners. She had one for the restaurant, colored red. One for her Job, colored blue. She was a Stewardess and would often be away for several weeks at a time. Lastly, she had one for her social life or lack thereof, Eric would muse - colored white.

"I've already held our monthly meeting with the staff at The Heart and Soul. They're appraised on the added changes to the menu, and prices," she continued.

The Heart and Soul Restaurant was their bread and butter. When his sister had first approached him about going into the restaurant business together, he'd been reluctant. He had a 'born stubborn, and almost impossible to alter view', is how she'd described it, several times, but he'd proved her wrong, as she'd managed to sign him up as a silent partner in the end. It was tough going at first but they stuck with it. Researching the market and networking in the right circles to eventually make it out of the red and into the black, though it had taken three years all told.

"I've also met with our lawyers and have got our recipes copyrighted. I've met with our accountants, and everything is looking lovely. All in all, I have to say we are blessed." Erica affirmed.

"Talk about a show off," Eric teased. He was rewarded with her laughter. Eric smiled at the sound, he loved his sister dearly. Due to their past hurts, Erica hardly ever laughed. When she did, it was just beautiful to hear.

"Don't be a whiney baby. I can't help it that I was born an awesome woman, blessed with the gift to multitask." She coughed lightly before whispering. "Unlike you."

Eric paused midway in putting on his black blazer. "Hey, I heard that, show your brother a little respect. You are a gift, baby girl, never forget that." There was a small pause. It was hard for Erica to receive compliments. Eric frowned, he knew it was due to their Aunt's verbal poisoning. "Sounds like you got everything under control," he praised, finally putting on his blazer.

"Of course. Never doubt it, babe." Erica replied confidently, perking up again.

"Of course not. You won't let me," Eric countered.

He heard her sniff proudly, "that's what sisters are for, to remind their brothers of important things, such as that." Erica sighed. There was a pause, filled with the sound of passing traffic before she went on, "you know; I've been getting the feeling, again."

Eric was still and speechless. The feeling; it was a gift or a curse but either way they both knew it meant their senses were telling them that something was going to happen.

"I can't shake it this time, it's stronger than ever. Please, be careful, Eric." His sister's voice had lost its usual bounce, now it trembled.

He was comforted by her concern for him but felt well equipped to defend himself. She often seemed to forget that he was combat trained though he had to concede that his radar had also been going off, lately. It was a sign that something was about to go down and that it was unlikely to be pretty. NWO, maybe? Eric prayed that it wasn't related to The New World Order but somewhere deep inside he knew it was.

"By the pricking of my thumbs, something wicked this way comes," he quoted from Shakespeare. Eric sighed, running his hand down his face in frustration. "I've been getting those feelings, too. I have a feeling something ugly is going to happen. I'm being alert and watchful, as always. And, I want you to be extra careful, as well. These feelings aren't always clear cut, Erica." Having reassured his sister of the care he intended to take, several times, he said goodbye.

Eric started the car; he made a point of looking both ways before pulling off and heading for I40, to start of his shift. Eric's thoughts turned to Rayna as he drove. He didn't like that at all. He wanted to be free from her pull. What was it about her? He'd dated a bevy of beautiful women, all of whom had been successful in their own right.

He pinched the bridge of his nose, a sign of tension, perhaps. Several of those relationships had proven to be quite messy. Eric was never one to lead women on, nor was he in the habit of using women. Right from the outset he'd be upfront, tell a woman that he was not ready to settle down. He was just looking for some good clean fun and some stimulating conversation.

Always the same straight-up approach, met with an often repeated pattern of events. At first, it seemed they were with the program but over time, with the seasons their expectations would change. It would become clear that they wanted to take the relationship to another level and the more he resisted, the more the guilt trip kicked in, leading to an inevitable end of the line. Rayna's aura had stayed with him, though. He'd never find another woman like her, even though at the time things got messy. Since, he'd placed himself on a dating sabbatical, something he'd managed to faithfully uphold for over a year and a half now.

As he swung the car gently into the police station parking lot, it occurred to him that you couldn't take your blessings for granted. He loved his job, what it involved and the way he did it. Time in the role had matured his instincts and he now felt as though he was in an ideal position to do his job to the best of his ability. His cell phone alerted him to an incoming call. It was Mike.

"What's up, Mike," Eric greeted warmly.

"What's up, Man. Look, I've got some good news. We've been invited to what I'm sure is going to be one of the biggest social events to hit the ATL." Mike sounded extremely enthusiastic.

"Sounds like fun," he replied dryly. His family and friends all knew he detested crowded social events; he felt like a caged tiger when he attended them.

"I knew you'd be excited. Sheila will be receiving the survivor's award, which we're both excited and nervous about."

"With good reason, considering her past experiences," Eric

concurred.

"Exactly. We've been advised that security will be provided due to the high profile, local and national electives in attendance. I've got to tell you, bro, we'd feel much better if you were there. Extra security. You know us. Love us. Would do whatever it takes to protect us."

"No doubt, man. You don't even have to ask me. I am there."

Mike sighed, "Thanks, man. I knew we could count on you."

"No thanks are necessary, we're family." As he spoke, Eric maneuvered himself out of the car and began walking towards the station building. "So, tell me more about this social function?"

Mike laughed, aware of Eric's distain for social events, "it's the What-a-Lady group. They're a support group for women who've suffered abuse. This is their first annual conference; their success rate has reached the hearts and ears of people across the world."

Both CNN and Headline News ran a feature on them, donations and support started flowing in. Their principle is to give recognition to their volunteers, those who strive to support women who've endured and survived abusive trauma. My baby's one of those chosen for recognition." Mike's voice rose with pride.

"Be sure to send me the particulars, I want to look my best." Eric replied half serious.

"As well you should, you know Rayna will be there, she'll be one of the award recipients as well, in fact."

Eric masked his uneasy surprise, "and you're telling me this, because?"

"Because, I'm your boy and am looking out for you," Mike cut in before Eric could respond. "I'm about to meet Mom for breakfast, you know how she is when I'm late."

Eric smiled with affectionate recognition, "indeed. Give her and Pops my love," he disconnected the call.

Eric was still smiling as he reached his office. He sat down at his desk, its scattered paperwork and half read reports seeming very familiar. In moments, his mind had returned to thoughts of Rayna. He remembered her smile and doe shaped eyes. By now he'd grown used to the odd palpitations that accompanied these thoughts.

The 'Lady's' event might be what was causing his radar to go haywire but either way he was going to be there, for his family. All the same, it didn't escape his notice that he was just a couple of days away from seeing Rayna's smile once more, from watching her stride elegantly across the room, hearing her soothing voice. Ugh, great, now he was becoming a stalker. He turned the computer on, resolving to put Rayna out of his mind for the rest of the day and knowing this was just wishful thinking.

* * *

A foul cocktail of pungent smelling odors assaulted his senses but he paid little heed. Drakus kept his head down, trying to blend into the shadows. He didn't need a watch to know that it would be daylight soon. His body was attuned to nature's rhythms. He looked up at the dark sky sprinkled with stars and cursed loudly. The little buggers always gave him the creeps. It was as if they taunted him with mysteries he could not behold. He cleared his throat and spat the contents ground ward.

"Hey! You arrogant fool. Didn't your mother teach you any manners?"

A gruff voice arose from somewhere close behind him. He came to a deliberate halt and looked slowly over his shoulder; dark meeting blood-shot ice blue eyes. The complainant swallowed profusely, his mouth suddenly going dry. He needed another shot of the cold hard liquor of which he'd already imbibed a little too much.

His hand itched in anticipation of raising the bottle to his chapped lips. His old frayed instincts were telling him, this one was evil. He took a good gulp, Dutch courage, to stave off the sense of intimidation. The eyes of the figure boring into him appeared to turn to stone.

His eyes maintained their focus, as he turned his body to face the drunkard. A patient smile touched his mouth as he briefly wondered what had caused this weak specimen to be brought so low. A justification, he re-told himself, why he had been chosen to lead Zion. Through his unforgiving leadership, weaklings like this would all be eradicated. It would be the survival of the fittest. Those who survived would breed a new generation of the athletic, intelligence and most importantly, obedient, who would rise up and rule.

He grimaced; there was that sense again, of momentous plans being placed on hold, and all because of a feeble girl. He growled aloud, the sound carrying in the air, causing a casual alley cat to leap from a dumpster and scurry into hiding. He took two deliberate strides towards the drunkard, summoned the phlegm from deep in his throat and spat it in the man's fearful face. Satisfied, he turned and proceeded to walk away.

The man attempted through blinks and gasps to wipe the thick sticky matter away, using his filthy pants to dry his hands. "Arrghh! You rat face," he almost fell forward into an unsteady stride after the dark figure. "Hey, you! I am talking to you. Don't ignore me. You think you're better than me?" bursting into a hysterical laugh, while almost tripping over his own feet.

"Well, you're not," breathing heavily and failing to keep up with the pursuant, he staggered against the dirty wall to keep from falling. His head was spinning, he was getting nauseous, a step away from relieving himself of his last meager meal but he managed to yell. "I'll not be disrespected. You're no better than I, dark one!" His voice grew louder, more infuriated, "things aren't always what they seem." Overcome with dizziness he crouched and began laughing mirthlessly. "I know your kind. And I also know you!" He sang the words.

The dark one stopped mid-stride and stood as if frozen to the spot. The flaps at the base of his full length black coat were cast aside by a sudden gust of wind. It was at such times, between assurance and who knew what, that shards of memory resurfaced. He was impervious to his mother's love; her hugs and kisses meant nothing to him, roused no emotions in him.

He remembered the actions of the woman but no connection with any effects of those actions. 'His eyes are so cold.' He recalled the overheard words of the woman, despair and fear coming across in spite of those attempts at motherly love. The day he'd returned home to find no mother there.

This was an often repeated sequence of recollection and playback of a worn tape. No mother and a note which read, 'The generational curse will never be broken. May God have mercy on your soul.' He read the words without understanding them but had retained and re-read the note over time. Even now, he did not entirely understand what was meant, just, that he was what he was. Left alone, he had to survive. He had survived. To keep going forward he had exercised discipline and control over himself, become highly focused.

Corbin had achieved all this without divine help – curse the thought. He was not going to put his faith in anyone but himself, and certainly not in a non-existent God. In the spiraling of time, his self-determination and resilience made sense. The purpose of his existence was made clear to him. He has been chosen to reside over the bringing forth of a new generation. Clearly, it was his destiny.

To the drunk, looking on, now silent, the shadowy figure

resembled a wraith. The notion of evil returned to his inebriated mind; is this what death looked like? Perversely, the thought tickled him and he fell victim to that uncontrollable laugher once more. "Was it something I said?"

He managed to yell out, between bouts of hysteria. He's like a large beast in hiding, the drunkard thought, dangerous to chase a wounded animal. As the dark figure turned once more; to look in his direction, Corbin suddenly seemingly to have sobered up. He watched apprehensively as the man raised his right hand, index finger extended in his direction; pantomiming firing a gun.

The movement caused the hairs on the back of his neck to bristle. He heaved himself from the wall and walked towards the dark silhouette. As he approached, Corbin drew close and spoke clearly, "they are growing restless, and even now they are seeking another. Boy, you have really messed things up." His smile was vindictive and the dark one, head lowered to shield his face, looked wounded, indeed. "Your problem is...you've gotten lazy, too assured in your own abilities. Overestimated the little ones."

There was a rustling, that Corbin could hardly detect, and then he felt a pressure squeezing his windpipe. Wounded but not defeated, the dark one had him by the throat and was pressing him up against the opposite wall. Corbin gasped, the dimly lit alley became dimmer and a haze began to fill his head.

Drakus – who in Corbin's eyes, now seeming even darker – lifted him almost off his feet. The stony black eyes darted across Corbin's face; for what, in Corbin's near death state, seemed to be an eternity. Corbin knew he was looking into the eyes of evil at that moment.

Drakus' eye were so dark you could hardly see the white. His, skin was itched with lines of harsh living. Corbin thought Drakus reminded him of the demented character in a movie he'd once snuck into see titled *Silence of the Lambs.*

"You should have kept your mouth shut when you had the chance," Drakus whispered menacingly. Corbin thought he suffered from a bad case of halitosis. But Drakus', breath nearly sent him to his knees. Drakus drew Corbin to him before slamming him back up against the wall.

Corbin grunted, seemingly hurt the piercing maniacal laughter erupted from him again. Once more, Drakus jerked him forward and rammed him hard against the dirty unforgiving surface. Sure enough, the laughter was abruptly stopped as Corbin began to wheeze.

"You like carrying messages, here's one for you, how does one beg for one's measly life?" Drakus remained quietly spoken but his venom was audible. Spittle was flying everywhere, some landing on the side of Corbin's left cheek.

Between bouts of heavy breathlessness, Corbin spat out words, "You...always...had a temper about you...even...as a child, Drakus."

Drakus' eyes widened in shock at the mention of his name from the lips of this stranger. Once again, he hastily scanned the face for any sign of recognition - nothing.

"Now, now, if you kill me...who will help you out of this fine mess?"

This did not sooth his savage soul, he applied more force, consolidating his grip on the man's throat and evoking a dry rasping sound from his mouth. He was not one to be toyed with. "You have less than five seconds, who are you?" He relieved the active choke hold, keeping the man pinned firmly against the bricks.

Corbin panted, "I thought...you'd want to...know, how I know...your name, first?"

"Five...Four..."

"Corbin...Corbin is who I am. I've been sent, tasked with

assisting you." He choked out.

"Who are you? Three…two…" Drakus began applying more pressure.

Corbin was beginning see stars. "The Forge, I've been assigned this task by The Forge." He squeezed out. Drakus heard the pathetic man's words but did not process them immediately. His surprise was followed by hope but not surpassed by suspicion. This is the one that The Forge had sent him as an aid? The Forge was another sect that had branched off from The Triune. Drakus frowned.

The three leaders were destroying Zion, he needed to take his rightful place as leader soon. The Forge left due to the Triune stifling rules and their poor end results. Drakus didn't trust The Forge either but was wise enough to understand he couldn't pull off what he had planned alone. Yes, he would need some help and why not accept the help of The Forge. For now.

Hope, was not lost then, but hope in the form of this lowly human being. A weakling such as this, sent to help him, a man of action. Word, quick to turn to rumor, was sure to have reached The Triune; things had not gone as he had expected. Who would have thought that Monica, that little brat, would connect with her sister and compromise his plans. Corbin sensed his chance and spoke with as much sincerity as he could muster, "it is true. I have been sent to help you assume your rightful place."

Drakus relinquished his grip but did not take his eyes off of the man in front of him. "Of course. I do not doubt The Forge. Doubtless, you have much to tell me."

Corbin nodded his head in agreement and began laughing. It was evident he was everything evil. Drakus turned without saying a word, confident the drunkard would follow. The time for Zion to rise has come.

* * *

The Heart and Soul restaurant, as one notable reviewer would have it - 'one of the finest in the Metro Atlanta area' - was as a usual on a Sunday night, oversubscribed by patrons. In addition to the full tables inside, people were prepared to stand patiently in line outside, queuing for a much sought after seat. Sipping from her glass of raspberry lemonade, Rayna sighed delighted by the tart taste and pleasant tickle in her throat.

She was appreciative of Philip's reservation. The restaurant had been expertly decorated, with no aspect of attention to detail having been neglected. Its exquisite design encouraged the eye to glide smoothly across the alluring space; ornate furniture and color matched walls bedecked with beautiful landscape paintings, and more modern splashes of artistic endeavor.

She took her time examining the familiar menu, something she always enjoyed; grilled fish, a variety of steaks, several pasta dishes, salad options and a range of appetizing pizzas. It was owned by a brother and sister partnership, so she'd been told, and though she'd been coming here for what seemed like years, she had never met them.

Phil's sudden return from making a private call; caused her to jump slightly; she had been lost in the ambiance of the place and had forgotten he was there.

"Hey, why the sad look? You seemed so happy a moment ago. If you don't like it here we can leave?" Philip looked around for their waiter.

"No, no. I love it here. I was just turning over some ancient memories," she shrugged a delicate shoulder. "Some things are just not meant to be."

He was experiencing it again, seeing her anew, which made him smile inside. He'd admitted to himself a while back that he was falling in love with her. Rayna was beautiful inside and out, and best of all, she seemed oblivious to it. She was unusual in appearance; her skin was the color of cinnamon, she had long wavy black hair, and raven wing lashes covered her large doe brown eyes.

Rayna was of average height and was what some would call 'curvy'. To him, she was just right. Rayna was full of energy, despite the long hours she worked and her heavy voluntary caseload. On Wednesday evenings she helped out as a coach, at the local chapter of, 'Mentoring Children of Divine Destiny', a program designed to enrich and improve the lives of children from deprived backgrounds.

A soft squeeze on her hand brought Rayna back to her present. Sighing softly, she warmly returned the affectionate gesture. Here we go, she thought. Foolish girl, why couldn't she feel something for this man? Philip was ideal-husband material. He was a practicing Heart Surgeon at Mercy Hospital. At the age of thirty three, he was the youngest physician there. They shared the same interests; theatre, museums, volunteering, and even a similar taste in books.

In the circumstances, the lack of a romantic tie was frustrating; most of the time she guarded what she felt or thought about him. Phil was in superb shape; his visits to the gym were paying off. He was broad shouldered, had piercing dark brown eyes and his skin was the color of smoothly blended milk chocolate.

Rayna recalled him telling her countless times, how he had to work triple hard to negate the color based stereotypes that abounded in the wake of affirmative action. He believed that some patients equated his young age with a lack of experience and so were reluctant to be treated by him.

"I feel like I'm competing with the surroundings to get your attention, honey." He leaned in closer, lowering his voice, "don't get me wrong, trust me, I am prepared to fight for you, I just need to know who or what I am fight against."

"You're not, believe me, you have my complete attention," Rayna inhaled deeply, she gave him a warm reassuring smile. She cupped his hands. She couldn't help but wish she could offer him more but the attraction just wasn't there. Her heart did not go 'pitter patter' in the face of his kindness and charm. Inside, hidden just out of her conscious sight, the reason for her withheld feelings was known. There was someone else who had captured her romantic imaginings, though she could not bring herself to think of or even say his name aloud.

Suddenly she felt a curious sensation that made the fine hairs on the back of her neck stand up. Philip seemed oblivious to any change. She casually looked around the restaurant for signs of anything out of the ordinary. There was an older couple, corner table, smiling lovingly at each other.

To their right, there were a younger looking couple; the woman seemed upset, she had her arms folded. Her companion out of choice or lack of attention didn't appear to have noticed her fiery stare. Rayna continued to peruse, feeling as if someone was watching her. She was aware that Philip was speaking but couldn't concentrate on what he had to say.

Chapter 2

He was in a bad way, something about the man and woman across the room was causing him to become out of character. Eric had been trained to control his emotions, to remain focused in the most perilous of situations. He remembered the drill, deep breath, 'one, two, three...' Then he noticed that the man had cupped the woman's hands in his and Eric was almost out of his seat before realizing his actions. Sitting back down, he closed his eyes briefly and concentrated. As a distraction he sipped his beverage and scowled; for the first time he wished it was something stronger.

Eric stilled as Rayna suddenly lifted her head, as if searching for something or someone. She's beautiful, he thought, inside and out. As she scanned the room be was torn between not wanting to be spotted and seeing the reaction on her face, if she did spot him.

He followed the news about her in the local paper. Recently she had been honored for her outstanding community work with the McLain Alumni Award of Distinction, at the Global AIDS Alliance in Atlanta. His heart had accelerated as his eyes had glimpsed the picture of her that had accompanied the article. She looked stunning in her fuchsia one-shoulder, mid-thigh dress, her hair an abundant cascade. 'Who'd escorted her to that function,' he'd wondered at the time.

Eric didn't think she'd spotted him but it was their laughter that bothered him now. He clenched his teeth again, the muscle in his jaw twitching. Best thing was not to look in their direction, he told himself but it was like trying to tell the sun not to shine. He had to look. Rayna took his breath away. She seemed so radiant, eyes twinkling with laughter, head tilted slightly to the side, her luxurious hair flowing down her slender back in waves.

Expelling a breath he wasn't aware he'd been holding, he slid deeper into his chair, his hand tightened around the stem of his glass. Eric recognized the guy with Rayna; he had come across him at Mike's wedding. He made a mental note to find out about 'Mr. Feel Good' as soon as he had the opportunity.

"Still hiding in the shadows, brother dear?"

Eric didn't bother to pull his gaze away from the object of all his distraction as he answered, "What can I say? I am a shadow dweller." He turned to look at Erica, "now sit down and let's get this meal started. You are late, again."

As expected she looked stunning in a green jeweled halter dress. Her caramel skin glowed. "Eric, please don't be mad with me. I had quite an episode trying to get here tonight," she implored.

It occurred to him that recently she'd been acting strangely. He hadn't bothered to enquire, knowing her fiercely independent nature; she'd just shrug off his concerns. "Sit."

The command had Erica folding her arms across her chest in irritation. She waited for him to look at her. As much as she loved him dearly, he could come across as quite mechanical and overbearing, though she knew that behind the steely veneer there was a loving man.

He'd had to put up with a lot, too much during their hellish upbringing which would have been enough to affect the outlook of anyone. He deserved a good woman to love him unconditionally, she felt, one who could see him for the true man he was and not as an opportunity to live a lavish life style.

The siblings exchanged looks, Erica raising one finely arched brow and sighing. They were as stubborn as each other, in the past their starring matches had gone on for days. He conceded suddenly, smiling and standing to pull a chair out for her. He bowed low at the waste courteously, "please, sit."

Erica was happy to oblige, she relaxed, kissing her brother's cheek before taking her seat. "Thank you. That is better. You know, I don't take kindly to being ordered around, Eric. You of all people should know this." She swiped away a stray lock of her hair as she settled at the table. "I just got a call from my supervisor confirming I'll be working out of town for the next couple of weeks."

She removed the slice of lemon from her glass of mineral water and her face responded to the sour taste as she briefly sucked on it. "So my dear loving brother, you'll have to attend next week's meetings." As a flight attendant, she was used to unusual shift patterns. Erica looked up in greeting, her eyes sparkling with delight, "hi, Vera. We have a great crowd tonight, I see."

Vera was a petite African American college student. She wore her hair in Singhalese twists that fell down to her waist. She was great with customers; many of their returning patrons made requests to be waited on by Vera.

"Ms. Miller," Vera's personality sparkled and shined. "We have a packed house every night. I can't say I blame them, our food here is sensational, there's the Thursday night Karaoke, that's helped tremendously to increase business." She spoke gleefully, "I don't know. It looks like this place may need to be added on to or you might need a Heart and Soul Two."

Eric started to speak but Erica cut him off, "I couldn't agree with you more. Chef Comerford was a God send, the place has been packed out ever since his arrival."

Comerford was a sought after chef of national renown. Erica hadn't expected him to take on the job as Head Chef but Eric said he'd accepted the position without hesitation, which made her wonder if he didn't own Eric one or two outstanding favors. Still, that was Eric for you, always saving the world, yet asking for so little in return. "Opening up a second restaurant would be another big step, but worth considering." She looked up at the bubbly petite waitress. "Thanks, Vera, for your thoughtful insight, we will keep everyone appraised."

Eric filed away Vera's suggestion. Actually, expanding the place wasn't a bad idea. They would need another manage, and he had an idea who she might be.

Erica briefly glanced at the menu before snapping it shut, "I think I'll try his latest recipe, the Maine Lobster Fondue Artichoke and Reggiano Cheese Ravioli, with butternut squash crème brulee and an Iced Tea for desert."

Vera nodded in acknowledgement, she did not write the order down. Erica had been amazed by this early on but soon discovered it was a trick of the trade, and something that several of the waiting staff had mastered.

"And you, Sir?" Vera smiled at Eric. "What will you be having tonight?" She exchanged a look with Erica, as Eric didn't answer her.

Frowning, Erica looked at her brother who was clearly distracted. He was staring at something across the room. She angled her head to try to see what had enraptured his attention but couldn't spot anything in particular.

As if sensing he was being watched, Eric finally answered. "I'll be having the Rosemary-encrusted Elysian Farm Lamb, Crispy Eggplant, and Swiss Chard, and a refill on my glass please, Vera." His gaze remained trained; he did not look down at the menu.

Vera sounded as cheerful as ever, "sure thing, I will return shortly with your orders." She nodded at them, before going to place their orders.

Eric's hazel eyes looked darker to Erica, indicative of a brewing storm, she felt. Once again she surveyed the heavily populated restaurant and once again she came up short. She kicked him hard under the table.

His gaze remained resolute but he whispered softly, "little one, you'd better have a good reason and I do mean, good, reason for assaulting a highly trained agent in a place filled with witnesses."

"Who are you looking at?"

"You," Eric replied softly, his attention suddenly returning.

Erica shivered under his direct gaze. Sometimes, her brother frightened her. Of course, she knew; Eric would never hurt her. It was just his moods could quickly shift from good to bad, without any warning. "I meant, before me. Don't be obtuse, brother dear." She was strongly tempted to throw a piece of her cheese biscuit at him, but the bite size treasure was just too delicious to waste. They held each other's stares, something they'd done since childhood - a 'twin thing' some had labelled it. Before long she was rewarded with a smile, she felt as though she'd won.

Rayna suddenly stood and Eric guessed she was going to the restroom. He jumped up, leaving the table and an astonished Erica, behind. He negotiated by fellow diners, smiling and nodding in greeting, while in pursuit of Rayna, noticing clearly now that she was wearing a purple drapey, button-through jersey shirt, knee length inverted pleated skirt, and that three inch heels adorned her feet. His heart accelerating at her beauty.

He was locked on to her, determined she wouldn't leave his presence without speaking to him first. It mattered not, she wasn't aware he was even in the building, a slight he was determined to fix. Rayna entered the ladies room; he could smell her lingering perfume. Inhaling, he leaned silently against the wall, and did what he did best. Waited.

Inside the restroom Rayna splashed water on her face. Try as she might she couldn't escape the feeling of being watched. She'd told Phillip she had a headache which was not a total lie because she did feel one coming on. She had suffered from migraine since she was a child; as an adult they'd tended to be triggered by stress. This place reminded her of someone. No, not someone, him. She had been doing great at forgetting Eric until moments ago when she had been unexpectedly assailed by memories of his smile and enthralling eyes.

Stop it, she told herself. "He'd made it perfectly clear that he didn't want anything to do with you, so let it go." She whispered. Rayna looked hard at her reflection. "Phil is a great guy and wants to be with you. Don't blow it, kid." She smiled in the mirror at the attempt she was making with herself to seal the deal.

Applying a second coat of her favorite MAC burgundy colored lipstick, Rayna smiled with confidence, replace the lipstick in her small purse she smiled wider. It was short lived, her heart betrayed her; as she opened the door and came face to face with a casual looking Eric.

Really? Did he have to be so fine? Rayna was not fooled, even in her heightened state of confusion and excitement, she sensed Eric's concealed tension. Rayna wanted to retreat back into the Ladies room, but held fast, she never ran from anything. She certainly wasn't going to start now. She raised her chin, defiantly. Eric smiled at the feminine challenge.

The intensity in his eyes arrested her, in the pit of her stomach there was a light airy sensation. She felt as though he could see her, the real her. She swallowed several times, managing to glance around to see if Philip was in sight, she couldn't see him.

Eric shook his head slowly, "don't worry, I won't keep you from lover boy," his words, were steely, softly spoken.

She knew his tone disguised the true intent of his words. What was his problem? Surely he wasn't upset with her for having dinner with someone else? He had set the rules and she was playing by them. "Well, that's good 'cause I wouldn't want to be rude and keep him waiting," she couldn't help but release a saucy smile as she started away from him.

"I'd never figured you for the preppy boy type. You are fire and he is ice."

Rayna's heart stopped, as he maneuvered slightly to obstruct her path. She wanted to run from him or to him, she didn't know which. His presence unleashed emotions that she could not prepare for and which had her leaping and falling, joyful and angry. She liked control and around this man all control was lost. Eric leaned in close, she could smell his cologne. Inhaling, Rayna prayed silently, 'please, Jesus, show me what I must do. If he doesn't want me, please give me the strength to resist him.'

Rayna cleared her throat. "That is kind of rude of you don't you think, Eric? You don't know anything about Philip…"

He cut her off, "Philip?" He stood legs braced apart and folded his arms across his chest. He did this to keep from gathering her into his arms. He wanted to hold her desperately, yet he knew he had no right to do so.

He was growing angry with himself. He had limited experience with matters of the heart and felt he might be badly mishandling the situation; offending or hurting her, neither of which were the intention. Her eyes watched him wearily, he would prefer lovingly. "Tell me, Rayna, does good ol' Phil have a last name?"

"That's none of your business," she was determined to give him nothing, information included, despite the magnetic pull she felt he exerted over her. Rayna knew Eric was the best at what he did, if he wanted he could have all the details on Phil by midnight. Fine, as long as it wasn't from her. She would never admit that she conducted her own private investigation on Eric. Thanks to Google, she was aware of Eric's many prestigious awards and his many sacrifices he made to bring the bad guys down. Rayna shook her head, a little peeved at all the risks he took for his partners, the man has probably seen the inside of hospital more than he did the police station. Rayna wondered if he sometimes put himself in the line of danger, to just end it all. The thought was frightening, so much; she took a step forward wanting to gather him in her arms, to take the pain away. Eric looked at her in question; of course he would notice her sudden movement.

"How long have you been talking to this guy? Really, he could be some kind of stalker." Eric admonished.

'Stalker', she examined the word. She didn't want to show it but his cryptic phrase rang home with her. It was only recently that her best friend, Sheila, had been the victim of someone the police had labelled a stalker. Shelia had told her just how harrowing the whole series of incidents had been, and how the lead investigating officer had suspected that her assailant was no ordinary fixated weirdo.

She'd said the officer had referred to the perpetrator as the 'dark one' or something similar. It had all seemed surreal to Rayna at the time but now she made a fleeting connection between Sheila's description of the officer and Eric. That monster was still out there somewhere, probably planning his next attack. The thought sent chills down her spine. She must have flinched because Eric was now gently rubbing her forearms as if to warm her.

Rayna looked up into his eyes, and immediately knew that was the wrong thing to do as she became spellbound by what she saw in them. This had her doubting herself, a feeling she detested. He was verbally saying one thing and acting in another way. Did he want her or not? Sighing softly, she stepped back, her headache was intensifying she realized.

"Look Eric, did you want something? I don't have time for this, this..." as her words faltered, she resorted to waving her hands weakly in front of her. "Whatever this is, you've made it painfully clear that it won't go anywhere, and I am not the type of woman to hang around where I'm not wanted. Life is too full for that." She remembered Phil, "I really must get back to my date. We were just about to take our leave for the night."

"You look exhausted, what are you doing to yourself?" Eric whispered. He'd concluded from the lines etched around her eyes and the occasional look of anguish flittering across her face, that she was unwell.

Rayna retreated, feeling slighted by the question, it was the last thing she had expected, 'You look even more beautiful than the last time I saw you,' would have certainly made her day. Still, he was showing concern, tenderness, and for a moment she wanted to give him anything he asked for.

"You really need to start taking better care of yourself. You're getting too thin," Eric chastised, and she immediately changed her mind.

With Eric she should have known to expect the opposite. Better off without him, she reminded herself. He was too complex, a Jigsaw-puzzle with too many pieces to fit together. He required too much effort and time.

"There you are. I was wondering where you went off to. And who is this?"

Rayna's stomach bottomed out. It was the woman she'd seen Eric with a couple of weeks ago. She was even more dazzling up close. Oh yeah, it was really time to be going; she was suddenly overwhelmed with envy, which made no sense, as she and Eric had never even had a relationship or been out on an official date. The emotions were strong but they'd come on too fast.

"Um, I really do have to be going. My date will begin to worry about me." Rayna brushed past Eric and practically ran from their presence.

Erica turned, hitting Eric on one broad shoulder. "Alright, what have you done now, Eric?"

He faced his irate sister in wide-eyed innocence and stretched out his hands, "what makes you think I did something wrong?"

Erica formed her mouth to say something.

Eric had second thoughts, "don't answer that."

When Rayna approached Philip she knew instinctively that something was amiss. He was on his cell, a frown marring his face. As she reached him he ended the call.

"I just got a call from the hospital; it seems I'm needed immediately. There's a patient with a severe heart condition. The on call attendant is in OR and the incoming patient needs surgery, fast. I hope you don't mind?" Phil was already standing; the bill she noticed was already settled.

Rayna shook her head, her eyes filled with concern. Philip loved that about her, she was the most compassionate woman he'd ever met. She was authentic and he wanted to make her his wife. He had thought that tonight would be the night he'd propose but something hadn't been quite right.

Philip kissed Rayna briefly on the cheek before departing hastily. She suddenly felt alone and exposed. The hairs on the nape of her neck bristled and she had that feeling again of being watched. She shrugged it off, ensuring that she kept her head held high and walked with as much elegance as she could muster, out of the Heart and Soul.

As she pulled away from the restaurant, she caught a glimpse of Eric in her rear view mirror. He was standing legs braced apart in his trademark style, on the restaurant's broad well lit wooden porch, starring in the direction of her car and her heart leapt.

Chapter 3

It was dark outside, not a star could be seen in the sky and even the moon hid its presence; just the way he loved it. The night seemed to be on his side. It was almost time; he had waited years for this stirring of the waters. Where others had failed, Drakus vowed to succeed. He had encountered setbacks, and learned from them. Another man would have given up; not him. He had been chosen for this.

Drakus got up from the filthy worn mattress. His skin itched, the result of multiple flea bites. With speed and micro precision he pinpointed one of the critters at rest on his arm, plucked it off, pincer like, and popped it into his mouth. He thought of his chosen mate. He should be angry at her, instead he was proud. It proved her strength and intellect. No one could hide from Zion as long has she had, particularly without help from those in prominent positions. It was all of her own doing, he smiled at the thought.

Drakus was now an outcast. Zion was seeking his life for failing to bring his intended bride before The Triune. He inhaled deeply, sucking up air before expelling it with determined force. Monica balanced him and the delay just made him want her all the more. Her resilience only served to prove that she was a worthy mate; breeder of a new world. Together they would create a better place, one comprising of the smartest, most disciplined and obedient.

Outside on the streets, many had long ago given up the prospect of ever doing well. For some, there was no redemption; their souls signed over to the devil, long since. They wore similar clothes, dark and tattered. In their hands were bottles of liquor and nicotine stained their grubby fingers. What a waste of flesh. Birds of a feather flocked together, he thought. They congregated, plotting their next crimes, he was sure of it.

The dimly lit hotel room was long past its prime, with peeling wall paper, frayed drapes and stains on the carpet. He peered through the mini blinds, the night was calling him. It had been his accomplice, bathing him in darkness as he had made acquaintances willing to sacrifice themselves to make Zion strong again.

His efforts had been exhaustive and he had found the 'willing and able' where ever they resided. They came from all stratus of society, all backgrounds: doctors, lawyers, police officers, and yes, clergymen. He heard the rustling coming from behind him but didn't turn.

Drakus's captive made another attempt to free herself. Hours had passed now and still she struggled to no avail. Her mind told her not to give up but her body had no more to give and could not obey. Her hands were bound tightly behind her back and had gone numb. In sheer desperation she had found herself wondering what it would be like to cross over to the other side.

How had this happen? Sure, it had been an extraordinary day. She and her boyfriend, Stan, were going to elope. They had decided that it was the only way to get around her parent's dislike of him. Stan was middle class - not good enough for their only daughter.

"It is useless to struggle," Drakus spoke firmly without looking at her.

She shook her head. The fatalistic words reminded her of her fear and caused her pulse to quicken, once again. "What do you want? Money? My father is a very wealthy man. He will give you anything you want. Just please, please don't kill me. I beg of you."

The sincerity of her pleas was like a drug to him, it gave him a rush that he found empowering. She reminded him of her mother, and this situation reminded him of the way in which her mother had pleaded. That was a long time ago. Now, as then, he exercised patience, saying nothing and awaiting her next pitiful utterance.

"Please. I beg of you, let me go," she began to cry softly.

He turned around slowly. Her eyes widened with fear and she swallowed until her mouth was dry; her eyes welling up with tears. She shook her head from side to side. "I don't want to die," her tears were unrestrained. Mucus coursed down her nose. At that moment, only life mattered. She wanted to live, and she was willing to do whatever it took to make that happen. "I don't want to die."

"What is your name?"

"Patricia," she whispered.

"When you woke up this morning, Patricia, what were your plans?"

It was obvious she wasn't expecting this question. She paused, trying to make out his features in the dim light. He was still, a statue that reminded her of the stone sculptures she had observed in the historic European cities she'd often visited. She had to clear her throat several times as she spoke, "I was going to work…after work, going to the gym." She stammered.

He already knew everything about her, down to the minute detail. He knew she had a birth defect, for example, an unsightly scar on her right thigh. He knew about her background, too. Montgomery and Alicia Hilliard came from new money; making billions from investments and real estate. Patricia was plain in appearance, with long braided shoulder length hair and oily skin that made her face glisten. He maintained his silence and this made her squirm all the more.

"You live in Buckhead in your palatial two point five million dollar mansion. A pity, your false and frivolous world deceives you. You thought you were safe from hurt and harm. Daddy and mommy lied to you, breeder. No one is safe in this world." He spoke deliberately, his movement hardly discernable. The headlights of a passing car raked the window and exaggerated his sinister shadow. For a moment, it was as if he was rising up to consume her and she tried harder than ever to make out his face. The lights gone, his shadow fading back, she was no wiser and no less afraid as he drew nearer to her.

Spittle stung her face as he closed in, "good job. If I did not know how masterfully you could weave a lie, I too, like mommy and daddy, would have believed you."

Fear induced nausea in her but she didn't want to anger him.

"You were not going to work this morning or to the gym. You were on your way to meet your pathetic little boyfriend." Drakus laughed mirthlessly at her shocked expression. "That is right, the one daddy forbade you to talk to. You ruined our plan when you and he decided to have relations." Drakus paused; he was savouring his words, probing at her Achilles heel.

Once, Patricia had strived to be the apple of her parent's eyes. Outside looking in, they appeared to be the consummate family. Unfortunately, the more she tried the less successful she seemed to be and the more her parents seemed to expect. When she volunteered to do charity work, they urged her to go further and become a host for lavish fund raising events.

The more their fame and influence grew, the greater the pressure she felt, and the harder it became to live up to their expectations. In the end it had all become too much for her and she had decided to just live her life as she felt fit; whilst maintaining the impression that she was part of the big, wealthy, happy family.

He adopted a caring tone, "I don't want to hurt you."

She was unconvinced, hadn't he already hurt her but she tried not to let her doubts show.

"I was merely saving you from making a bad decision. Your boyfriend, Stan, he was not in love with you. He knew at 18 you would become a trust fund baby. Isn't your 18th birthday tomorrow?"

"You are lying! Why should I believe you?" Her outburst surprised her and coming to her senses, she sought to tone it down. "I mean, I don't even know who you are." She was instantly aware of some sort of change in the creature as a result of her words; had his eyes widened, brightened?

The little minx had fire in her after all, he mused, drawing back from her, an odd contorted smile crossing his mouth. He pulled roughly at a draw of the ancient looking wooden desk to one corner of the room and withdrew a red folder, the contents of which he tipped onto the grubby carpet in front of her. She was caught off guard by his actions but now starred down at something even more disturbing. Pictures of Stan, were they really pictures of Stan? Yes, it was undeniable. Stan and another woman, holding and kissing passionately.

"It could be an old picture. Before me," she found herself saying, not wanting to give anything away to her captor but inside she felt sick, betrayed, humiliated. Had everything her self-righteous parent's had said been true about her intended. She felt as though she was falling into a pit. Stan had been her anchor, her link to survival, what did she have left now?

Drakus delighted in her emotional turmoil; control a person's heart and you control their mind. Within two strides he was behind her. Kneeling he placed his hands on the ties that bound her wrists and she flinched.

"Please, I am trying to help. I am going to untie your hands," he sounded concerned now. "I want to talk to you. I have a proposition. I am offering you a chance to avenge yourself. A chance to get back at those who hurt you. To exact vengeance." While he spoke he untied.

Patricia's arms dropped in relief as she felt the circulation returning to her hands. What was worse, she wondered, what was worse? She didn't know whether she should laugh or cry. This situation was unreal. The discovery that Stan was only using her was equally devastating, and the fact that her parent's had been right all along, was no less comforting. She grasped at her wrists, right hand squeezing the left, left hand the right, whilst she began rocking back and forth, looking more twelve than eighteen. "I don't understand. Who are you? Why are you telling me all this?"

There it was; the tiny gap he sought to exploit. "I only want to help you, child. I detest people who hurt others. You try to do right only to be done wrong. I feel your loneliness. Like calls to like." He remained behind her so as not to detract from the soothing nature of his voice. He knew he had her, when she leaned back into him. He smiled in victory.

Her eyes were dry now; all cried out, she simply stared straight ahead.

"With me you wouldn't have to worry about anyone ever hurting you like that again, sweet Patricia. With me there is only love and kindness." He dropped his voice lower. "Come to me; walk with me, away from your loneliness and into a world of unity, acceptance and peace. Aren't you tired of being alone, hiding the true you. With me, you won't ever have to hide yourself. I will always accept you for who you truly are."

Something about the sound or could it be the phrasing of his words was calling to her; replacing the terrible way she had often felt about herself, with a simple solution, a way out.

Drakus sensed the powerful workings of his concoction, drink it in, my dear, he willed silently, drink it all in. "People can be so frivolous. Not so, me. I am not blinded or beguiled by the complexities of this world. I can see what is needed and will do what it takes to make things better. A new world order will be brought about, child. Join us, be free." He stood and moved slowly in front of her, catching her dormant gaze. "Come to me," he urged gently, reassuringly.

She responded, rising steadily as if in a daze and looking directly at him, a sad look of defeat in her eyes. "What do you need me to do?" She asked quietly. Drakus smiled evilly, nodding his head with approval.

Chapter 4

Ever since he'd been a child, Philip had known he'd become a doctor. The pathway to his profession had been laid down by two generations of Stephens before him. As a Cardio Thoracic surgeon he had pursued a similar route to that of his grandfather. His father had been a family doctor. The two men who'd gone before had also passed down their determination to succeed, it wasn't good enough to be qualified; they'd asserted that you had to be the best. At thirty seven, he still wasn't sure he'd achieved that accolade but he was content that he was well on his way.

Dressed in familiar scrubs, he was totally prepared for the critical work that lay ahead of him. In God he placed his trust, as often, he knew, so did those he operated upon. This time his patient was a frail young woman, slight of frame and clinging on to life. He felt as he often did, that hers was – his - need. Even now, seven years in to becoming a surgeon and with all his training and skill to help them, he still didn't understand why people had to suffer.

His ability to contribute to saving lives was in contrast to the pain and death he had witnessed along the way. At times he became overwhelmed and when this happened he became withdrawn and unreachable by others. He felt that he had to do this in order to stay sane.

Many times he had felt himself tied to the proverbial cross; many times he wanted desperately, to be free. Calm would always settle over him eventually and then he would once again accept that he was just a man, with limited and sometimes no, answers.

He was an instrument on assignment to help meet the need of others and he vowed to do so with every fiber of his being.

As he went through his final mental preparations, Philip felt the familiar warm tingling sensation in his hands. It began in his fingertips and spread evenly, settling in his palms. He remembered when he'd first experienced this sensation. He'd been playing baseball in the park. His baby sister, Maureen, had been there although she'd have been having more fun if he'd been pushing her on the swings.

It had been a game his team, The Lion Gate, were determined to win, as for the last few weeks they had been losing to their rivals, The Hurricanes. As he stepped up to take his position, he felt confident in the belief that he was going to hit the ball out of the park and ensure his team's victory. As he gripped the bat in anticipation he felt a sense of foreboding but was quick to shake it off.

He wiped the sweat from his brow, switching the bat from his left to right hand and hitting the ground with it three times, before settling it into his left hand. He swung into the air, testing the feel of the bat. He felt ready. Looking into the eyes of the notoriously skilled pitcher, Jason McFadden, he swallowed hard.

He'd heard talk that Jason was destined to be a professional one day but Philip dispelled any doubts in his own ability. He had been practicing and praying hard in preparation. He recalled Jason throwing the ball and forcing himself to remain calm but he swung clumsily. Everything seemed to happen in slow motion as he stumbled and felt the bat connect, followed immediately by a collective gasp and screams from the onlookers.

His coach ran onto the field screaming for anyone to call the ambulance and he stood there frozen and in disbelief. His eight year old sister lay haphazardly on the ground, blood was coming from her mouth, her eyes were wide with shock and her little body was convulsing. He wanted to reach out to her but he couldn't move. His mother's screams could be heard in the distance. His sister's movements ceased and she became still.

"She's not breathing!" Someone shouted.

A big boned woman knelt down and leaned in to listen to the girl's chest. She rolled the child onto her side. More blood ran from her mouth and she used some paper napkins to wipe away what she could. Then, letting the motionless child fall gently back, she began mouth to mouth before commencing chest compressions.

"Did anyone call the paramedics?" A woman shouted.

"How did she get on the field? Where is her mother?" A man's voice bellowed.

Philip began to feel a tingling sensation in the palms of his hands; they were itching so badly that he began to rub them up and down on the pants of his baseball uniform. Tears streaming down his face, he attempted to kneel beside his sister but was ushered to keep back by the woman now administering to the lifeless child.

"I'm sorry, I'm sorry," he kept repeating.

It was a hot day and the woman was sweating profusely, yet she persisted. As she worked her lips moved fast and she emitted little utterances. "No weapon formed shall prosper…" Suddenly she looked up and he gasped aloud. Her eyes were bright, a fusion of light brown shades that seemed to shimmer and this captured his attention completely. He felt as if he knew her, although he could not remember meeting this woman before.

"She is my sister," Philip heard himself say.

The woman smiled, briefly nodding before turning her gaze back to the girl and continuing her vital work.

"She is not going to make it," he heard someone cry out.

"Please be quiet, Martha! If you want to talk, say a prayer, otherwise shut your trapper. We need positive energy now." A man's voice responded.

Seconds later, a soft prayerful murmuring had begun.

Philip had somehow managed to get to his sister's side now, and was holding her cold hand, his palms still tingling. They were so hot; they felt like they were on fire. Taking her hand in his, it felt as though he was passing something, some life force of himself onto her.

"I am with you little one. Just relax and believe."

He heard the woman's reassuring words and his heart almost leaped from his chest at the small calm voice.

"Remain focused, child. Your sister has need of you."

He could hear the ambulance siren advancing in the distance and he clung on to his sister's hand. He willed her to open her eyes and then a miracle happened. Maureen opened her eyes, her startled gaze roaming over the crowd who became silent and spellbound for a moment.

Maureen closed her eyes briefly and when she opened them again she was clearly restless with the pain. The woman held her to her breast and offered words of comfort. It seemed to work as Maureen's body became restful in her arms.

Shortly the paramedics had arrived and taken charge of the situation. One was a tall willowy blond man who began to bark out orders. The other was a short rotund man. He began to hook up an oxygen mask. Eventually, with care and attention, they lifted the child onto the gurney and transported her to the waiting ambulance.

His mother, still sobbing, walked with them and Philip trailed slowly behind in a daze.

As they reached the waiting vehicle his coach approached them, "its ok, Ma'am. I will take care of him. You focus on one thing at a time."

As she climbed into the ambulance, his mother nodded

through her many tears, mouthing the words, 'thank you'. The ambulance door's closed loudly and it accelerated, taking his sister and mom to the hospital. He looked around for the woman who had been such a brilliant help but she was nowhere to be found.

His sister had survived that terrible accident physically and despite the reconstructive surgery she had endured, the scars were barely noticeable now but inwardly he felt she'd been forever changed by the unfortunate episode.

The memory faded and he became aware of his imminent duty to the young girl on the operating table before him. 'Who are you little one? Where are your family and friends?' He asked himself.

He waited silently, willing her to move her fingers or for the fluttering of her eyelashes. He'd experience these things before, albeit rarely, still, his faith remained great.

Sighing he looked up at the clock signaling time to commence the procedure. He felt the weight of his responsibility press in, her life, his hands. Would he ever feel comfortable with these feelings? He offered up an earnest prayer for guidance and healing, taking a deep breath before beginning the operation.

Chapter 5

The young girl walked for what felt like hours and yet she didn't feel tired. She had no idea where she was and didn't care. She was feeling a great peace. She did miss her cat but prayed that he was all right. Up ahead a huge Chestnut tree held her attention; it was surrounded by a bed of soft lush red roses. They were majestic to look upon. She had never seen such vibrant roses. Their beauty beckoned her onwards and she broke into a run, her joyous laughter trailing in the wind. As she reached the stunning flowers, she bent to inhale their sweet perfume.

While savoring the delightful smell, she noticed a brook up ahead and rushed towards it. Standing at the edge of the clear, gently flowing water, she observed her reflection. Her face looked the same but she felt different somehow. Was it the white clothing? She found it strange that she was dressed in white from head to toe; white being her least favorite color.

She knelt down and briefly dipped her hand into the pool, feeling its coolness to touch and watching it ripple. As the water settled back to stillness she noticed something move behind her and leapt quickly to her feet, looking around. She saw no one. I must be going crazy, she thought, shaking her head softly and laughing aloud.

Resting for a spell she slumped down under the majestic chestnut trees and took in her surroundings. Everything seemed so bright and peaceful. Where was everyone? Suddenly she felt like, "Alice in Wonderland", minus the white rabbit, she mused.

"Who are you little one? Where are your family and friends?"

The faint words made her cry out loud, she stood frantically and looked around her. "Who said that?" Turning as she spoke, "where am I? And how did I get here?" Her query met silence. "Am I going mad?" She was captivated by the serene beauty of the brook; the still calm of the scene of which she found herself a part. The peace of the environment soothed her and dispelled any panic or fear. She found herself walking towards the welcoming waters.

A warming sensation coursed through her body and she could have sworn she felt something touch her forehead; she was surprised and perfectly calm. She closed her eyes and reached out a hand to touch the same spot on her head forehead.

"Hello."

The voice was warm and caring. This time she did not turn to see where it came from, choosing instead to close her eyes. "Who are you?" She asked blindly.

"Who I am is not of import. You are in need, have been for a while. I've been trying to connect with you for quite some time. You're a stubborn one, for sure." The voice advised.

As she opened her eyes she was greeted by bright light; so bright it obscured everything else. She was not disturbed and remained relaxed. Her eyes began to acclimatize and she could make out the shape of a man's face. The image did not crystalize but instead remained a bright glowing blur; the harder she looked, the brighter the light became.

She opted to observe her surroundings and found she appeared to be in a vast empty field; the grass an intense green, the sky a pristine blue. It was an immaculate site and it inspired awe and wonder in her. As she attempted to bring the figure back into focus, she was struck once more by the immense blinding light and lowered her eyes.

"My stubbornness has kept me alive all these years," Victoria shrugged nonchalantly. She felt the intensity of the stranger's gaze upon her.

"Yes, you are still alive. It is not your time. That is why I came to you. To tell you that your assignment is not over, yet. There are others out there, who are in great need of you, Victoria."

Victoria eyes widened. "How do you know my name?" She looked around. "And, where am I? Why do I feel like I've been here before, when I know I have never been here?"

"I know all that there is to know about everyone. But that is not of import, now. Time is of the essence. You need to willingly return to your body. You are fighting the healing process. There is one now who is fighting for you." The stranger's voice was low and absorbing.

"Forgive me, but I find that hard to believe. No one has ever fought for, me, ever." Her voiced hardened with anger. "I have been on my own for most of my life, and those who did help me, ended up wanting something from me in the end." Victoria wanted to walk away at that moment, but found she couldn't move. She looked up at the stranger, fear sneaking its way into her. Who was this man?

The stranger lay a gentle hand on her shoulder and she felt at peace once again. A sense of deep satisfying calm came over her and she never wanted the feeling to end.

As if reading her mind, the stranger shook his head. "I tell you that you cannot stay here" He reiterated. "It is not your time. Believe me when I tell you, that you will find the joy and completion you've been seeking. You've come too far, endured too much to give up now. Go back, child, go back and complete the work for which you were chosen."

Victoria starred out over the picturesque field and reveled in its serenity. It was calling to her; beckoning her to stay in this place of peace. The cold ache of loneliness was gone. There were no hunger pangs and no worries. Why would she want to return to a world filled with angst and sorrow?

"I am sorry but I can't. I just can't," she stood there trembling as she awaited his reaction. In the soft kindness of his tone she found every reason to do as he asked but she was afraid to return to that place of pain.

"You have no idea what will happen if you don't return to complete the cycle. You must return. I do understand your reaction but you need to have courage, steer away from selfishness." His voice was consistent, even. "You are needed back there, so are the others."

Others? She silently questioned.

"You suffered many losses, and yet were strong enough to continue living. The others are not as strong; they will need some assistance along the way. That assistance will come from you, one of the chosen few. The Remnant."

The force of her reaction to these words took her by surprise, "what are you talking about?" Shaking her head vehemently in denial, she tried to gain control over her anger. "I don't want to be a part of any Remnant. What or whoever that is. Look, I'm tired, so tired of the running, hiding, surviving. And, you want me to help those who are less strong, well, and tough. If they want to give up, then more power to them, because I have my own problems to worry about." She spoke with all the conviction she could muster.

The stranger met her outburst with an agreeable nod. Victoria silently wondered if he was capable of getting angry. His silence was louder than any words. In the silence Victoria examined herself, upon introspection,--finding someone, hurt, lost and angry. It was true, all her life she'd been on her own. No one ever reached out a finger to help her; all that she had, she had gained on her own terms, through her own tireless efforts and determination.

"You are connected," he waved his hand and a translucent moving image appeared from nowhere, at first it was unstable but finally it steadied and grew clearer. In this vision she could see the bright sun; clouds like cotton candy dotting the clear blue sky. The ground was covered with people from all walks of life, standing, smiling, chatting, and laughing. There were children playing freely, and animals. Dogs chased one another across open ground. Birds of different varieties swooped and called across the sky. It reminded her of a great park - she had always loved the park, a place she'd found endlessly comforting in the past.

The stranger waved his hand again and the vision faded becoming enveloped in darkness. She felt the sudden tumultuous flip-flop of her emotions, a dramatic slide from joy and happiness to concern and despair. It caused her to panic and she wanted to scream at the stranger to stop but she was paralyzed.

"Don't be afraid, little one, I am not foretelling of your ultimate destination but simply making you aware that such a place exists. Those who are sent to that place can never return. Their cries for release are never heeded. That is why The Remnant was dispatched to help guide others away from ending up in this place."

The light flared up again, she could see nothing and when her eyes readjusted he was no longer present.

Chapter 6

Corbin stepped out into the bright sunlight and frowned immediately. He hated the bright light bombarding his senses with pain that took the form of a mind numbing migraine. He was a child of the dark - 'the darker the merrier', one of his choice phrases.

As he reached the corner, he pulled out a small flask from his back pants pocket and took a quick swig before hastily replacing the vessel, and retrieving his cell phone. Once the call had connected he spoke clearly into the device, "our seed has been planted and is about to grow."

"Good," there was a hesitation on the end of the line. "And Corbin?"

"Yeah?" Corbin frowned impatiently.

"This season is upon Zion. We don't have room for error. Everything must be followed in precise order. No deviations can be made at this point."

Corbin frowned deepened. He didn't need to be told how dire the situation was, he knew what was required. "Yeah, yeah. I understand. I want to remind you that I want this just as bad as you do. I will do my part; you needn't worry about me…Sir. The time for Zion is here!"

"Good." The call was terminated.

He exchanged the cell phone for the flask, taking a satisfying slug and noting to his dismay that the vessel would need to be recharged before long. He continued towards the train station, somewhere he had frequented often in the past. He liked the grand scale of the place; somewhere you could blend into regardless of your state of sobriety.

The station also facilitated one of his treasured pursuits - people watching. He liked to watch people and take note of their habits. People were, he'd concluded, creatures of habit. Knowing the habits of those he observed, he felt, gave him a kind of superior power over them. As he watched, he studied and learned. Through his many observations he had discovered that the world had indeed evolved into a lackadaisical place. It was time for a change, to eradicate the cowards, the weak, the feeble minded.

In the station's enormous lobby he took up position near an unremarkable looking poster that had been posted on a side wall, and began his observations. Within a short period of time he had identified a target. Straightening up he began to follow a young girl that he'd spotted earlier. At that stage she'd been texting on her cell phone and he had noted how oblivious she'd appeared; all the better from his point of view.

As he trailed his victim he patted his hidden flask and salivated at the prospect of another stiff drink. For that he needed cash, something he hoped this ignorant young girl would soon provide. In robbing her he would be providing a valuable lesson, he felt, you should always pay attention, as you never knew who might be watching you.

* * *

"Code blue. Code blue. Code blue." The words echoed loudly over the speaker.

Philip had heard these words countless times before and had always dreaded them. Subconsciously, he knew that he could face such an incident any day but this knowledge did not make the prospect any easier to bear. Here and now, he wanted to scream and to hit the wall at the unexpected turn of events. He rapidly replayed the moments leading up to this point in his mind. He'd made a precise incision, opening up the chest wall to reveal the woman's vital organ. Only, he'd found the condition of her heart hard to comprehend.

It had been greatly enlarged, the result of coronary artery disease, he'd concluded - by far one of the worst cases he'd ever encountered. The only thing that astonished him more than this discovery was the fact that the unidentified woman, on whom he'd been operating, was alive at all. Then, the heart monitor had gone off making a dreaded continuous beeping sound, reminding him that time was of the essence.

The girl's heart was drowning in fluid, one of her left lung had collapsed and she needed a chest tube; what a mess. For the umpteenth time Philip wondered how she had survived this long? The sound of the heart monitor changed, replaced by a monotone shriek, she'd flat lined.

"I need that defibrillator ready for use, like yesterday, Nurse Porter. Increase oxygen intake, now. Prepare to resuscitate."

The supporting surgical team worked efficiently and the defibrillator was brought up. "Hurry," he urged firmly.

Nurse Porter glanced sharply at him. He never commanded, he simply directed – his words - and sure enough that was a command if ever she'd heard one.

Philip was aware that every second counted, they had to get the heart pumping again in order to restore the supply of oxygen and prevent brain damage. He worked skilfully to position the shock pads. "Clear," he instructed, waiting a split second before applying the pulse of electricity. The woman's body convulsed but the heart did not restart. He repeated the procedure to no avail. He placed the pads to one side and began to massage the heart with his left hand, willing it to beat. He paid no attention to the distractions around him and concentrated all his efforts on saving her life. All sound faded and his focus narrowed down; if this moment was the darkest hour then somewhere ahead of him there was light. He was sweating profusely, the salty drops stinging his eyes before someone dabbed at his forehead.

The warming sensation in his hands was causing them to itch and burn. It was a clear indication that he should use his gift of healing, something he normally only reserved for private consultations. This situation presented him with a real dilemma, how could he reveal his power to heal in front of the assembled surgical team, and hope to keep it from leaking out to the press. His imagination worked over time and he saw the lurid headline in the local newspaper - 'Certified surgeon to be certified'. All the while he remained calm and offered up a silent prayer.

The sensation did not abate but instead spread as a trickle of heat up through his arms, across his chest and over his entire body. All the while he continued with the heart massage despite the lack of a response and the growing sense of hopelessness. It was all too much and he stopped abruptly, to the surprise of those gather around watching him, waiting on his every move.

"Call the time," he instructed.

Nurse Porter looked at the huge clock above the operating table, "11:52 am."

They'd been trying to revive her for six minutes but it seemed like an eternity. There was no sign of dissent in the room, they were united in the sense that he, they, had done all they could but this did not dispel the sense of failure. The sensation of heat that had swept his body, waned now, eased quickly and he felt dejected.

"Doctor Stephens?" Nurse Porter's coffee colored eyes were fixed earnestly on him, "you did all you could for that young woman. Her heart was beyond salvation, I'd say it was a miracle that she came in here breathing in the first place."

In normal circumstances the protocol would have been to deliver the bad news to the decease's family members but he was acutely aware, that there was no next of kin to inform in the case of this young woman. He watched as the nurse covered the body with a crisp white cotton sheet. He looked around the sterile operating room, once again questioning himself; questioning if God really did always hear him. He shrugged in defeat.

"I'm going to clean up and get out of these scrubs."

Patting his arm awkwardly the nurse turned and exited the operating theatre, followed by the other members of the team. He wished he could walk away as easily, over the last few years he had tried but something just wouldn't let him go.

In that instant, the healing sensation returned to his hands and he felt compelled to act. Hastily he removed his surgical gloves and cast them to one side before lifting the sheet that covered the lifeless body. He lost no time, re-accessing the vital organ and commencing heart massage. Everything fell away from him; time ceased to exist, the clock ticking on the wall meant nothing. Something had taken him over. He worked and focused, concentrating so hard that he almost missed the first signs, as the heart began to pulsate almost indistinguishably at first.

There was the sudden memory of his injured sister lying on the ground, of the bat in his hand, and the sight of the blood emerging from her delicate mouth. These visions came to him as flashbacks, whilst in his hands he felt the young woman's heart begin to pump more regularly; it was beating again.

He did not hesitate, hitting the 'call' button before quickly scrubbing his hands and forearms, drying thoroughly and pulling on a replacement pair of gloves. The startled team members, none more so than Nurse Porter, were soon at his side once more, and working with frantic professionalism alongside him to complete the procedure they had started earlier.

"We've been granted a miracle ladies and gents," he declared. "Let's take full advantage of it."

Chapter 7

The control he exercised when calmly closing the door to the open plan office was at odds with the way he felt inside. Standing at his desk, Eric gave the impression of looking over case papers while paying no attention to their contents, such was his preoccupation. Everything he felt, thought, dreamed even, related to that woman. His attempts at pushing her out of his mind had clearly failed, judging from the emotional waves that had been generated since he'd seen her at the restaurant.

That had been the trigger for the flood gates to open, unleashing a mixture of unwanted memories. He could kick himself for following her out onto the porch that night. Now, he had another unwelcome memory to add to the pool; that of her getting into her car and driving away from him without another so much as another word. What more proof did he need that she wasn't interested? Why couldn't he get the message?

Eric sat down firmly in his chair, leaned back hard and propelled the air of frustration through his nostrils. He closed his eyes for want of rest, only to open them again rapidly when all he saw behind his closed lids was her. Rayna. Perhaps he shouldn't deny her. Perhaps she was genuinely meant for him. After all, fate had returned her to his life. Why now?

The day he'd first met her came into his mind. She'd been out jogging in heavy wind and rain. They were the sort of conditions other people would try to avoid but there she was, striding along regardless, a vision of beauty. He'd been cruising along in his car but his destination had become unimportant because he'd felt compelled to follow her. As he tailed the beautiful stranger, the voyeuristic nature of the situation had crossed his mind. What was he doing taking a detour to follow this lovely creature? Yet, in spite of his reservations he had carried on his pursuit. Eric's mind was racing ahead to how he could manage to keep tabs on her while not making it too obvious.

As Rayna slowed he came up alongside her. He noticed the long dark tresses of her hair bound by a thick braid, and took it as an indication of mixed linage. A squirrel zigzagging on the path ahead of her had to scramble out of her way. She ran with great determination, he thought, nothing could stand in her path.

As she strode he noticed the frantic movement of her mouth and it occurred to him that she might be insane. Had she been hurt by something or someone, he wondered. In the end, Rayna allowed him to escort her home. During the short drive to her home, he learned some pertinent details about her. That she was an Attorney, she loved jogging, and reading and more importantly, that she was also single. Why did he have to love that part the most? Smiling Eric allowed the memories of that day to resurface.

Lightning lit the sky, followed by the booming sound of thunder. Rayna screamed, tripping over the fallen debris. Landing flat on her stomach in the pouring rain, she laid there stunned. It was too much. Her falling in the storm was the last straw. The dam of false strength she had erected for so many years had broken. Like a tsunami, her tears of hurt flowed. She began to cry fast and furiously. From her low position, she looked up at the dark grey sky. The rain continued to pelt at her, the wind continued to pull at her long tresses, and she ignored all these outside interferences.

Her heart went into overdrive, as pent up emotions began to surface. In her fury, she began to pound the ground in sheer frustration. Rayna was angry, angry at her choice of becoming a mother being taken away from her. Barren. She would never know what it was like to physically carry a child. When she was young she suffered from a disease that caused damage to her fallopian tubes. Rayna thought after all the years past, she had accepted that harsh fact. But sometimes like now, the hurt was still raw and painful.

The rain continued and she purged herself, finally confessing that she was hurting. Rayna had suffered a setback, but vowed she would make it through her personal storm. The rain was refreshing. It was washing the fast falling tears from her eyes. Turning over on her back, Rayna closed her eyes. The rain continued to fall, washing her. As he realized he was drifting along far too slowly, he had injected a pulse of acceleration into the vehicle and at this moment the woman seemed to lose her balance and trip over.

His reactions were quick as he swung the car into the next available space at the curb but Eric did not leap out to her aide, instead choosing to observe what would happen next. When after a couple of minutes she hadn't moved, he found himself overly concerned. His heart beat had quickened and he was conscious of his breathing. After another minute he had opened the car door and ran over to where she lay. The wind whisked up in gusts and the rain continued to pour down as he knelt at her side.

A dark shadow fell over her, causing Rayna to scream out. She turned back over on her stomach and began to crawl away from her would be stalker. Sure, she had a problem, but she wanted to live to deal with it. "Help me! Someone help me!" she screamed. He had witnessed Rayna's breakdown. His first instinct had been to run to her, but something staid him. He simply watched her. Hurt recognizes hurt. Even in the storm, he saw her hurt. When she cried out, it was all he could do not to get out of his car and wrap her in his arms. He knew the healing process well.

The number one key to healing was to release the hurt. Right now, standing over her, he had to make her realize he was not the enemy. "That is what I'm trying to do, help you. Ms. uh, look, are you certifiably insane?" His voice sounded oddly amused. Outraged, Rayna stilled. Turning around, she was about to let him have one good lashing before their battle ensued. She froze, because this man was intriguing. He had skin the color of rich mocha. Broad shoulders, enhanced by the black leather jacket he was wearing. His eyes were hazel.

Then he smiled, and her heart leaped. Then he moved. Then she moved. "If you come near me I will use this." She held one hand out defensively. The stranger looked at the pitiful weapon and laughed. It was one of those deep belly laughs, which made you want to join in, even when you didn't get the joke.

Rayna had to bite down hard on her lip to refrain from laughing too. This was no laughing matter. She was feeling like a dunce. "Yeah, I would definitely say that you are certifiable. Pity you're so beautiful too." Rayna frowned, suddenly bothered. Oh, come on now. Did his voice have to sound so, so…Barry White? It took a moment for the stranger's words to register. She could not believe what he just said. Not the 'certifiable' comment, she would deal with that later. The 'beautiful' comment. Sure, she had been told she was beautiful countless times by men and women, because she was fierce when it came to her appearance.

She wasn't a frivolous person, she was quite frugal actually, but she had an image to live up to as one of Atlanta's most successful attorneys. It was a hard profession, even more so considering she was a woman. Her high-powered suits made her feel in charge. Everything had to be in place. Order was her place of comfort. However, the compliment coming from this man affected her differently. His words made her proud to be a woman. Not liking the feeling of losing control, she felt herself becoming angry. Rayna was certain she looked like some wet stray off the street. Yet, he claimed to see the beauty in the storm.

Eric laughed as he witnessed the myriad of emotions crossing Rayna's face. The sound was beatific, causing her stomach to flip flop. Her rescuer gently threw up his hands. "Look. I promise not to hurt you. I just want to help, that's all. Look, you can come to my car and use my mobile phone to call someone to help you if you like." He nodded at the meager weapon in her hand. "And you can put your weapon away." Rayna felt her face burning with embarrassment.

She quickly put the ballpoint pen in her sweat pants pocket. "I went jogging and got caught in the storm," she stated, scrambling to her feet. Rayna was so cold, that her teeth were chattering loudly. "Look, this is ridiculous, you're drenched through and through, and you're freezing." Eric reasoned. "You can catch pneumonia is this weather. Allow me to take you home. If it makes you feel safer," Eric nodded toward her pen. "you can even keep your weapon pointed at me." Rayna hugged her arms tightly around herself, wanting to hide the pen. "I give you my word that I will not harm you." He waited.

Rayna sighed; it was ridiculous how she got caught in this rainstorm. Maybe he was her hidden blessing in the storm. She sighed again and the stranger smiled. "Oh, all right..." Before she could finish her sentence, he purposely approached her. Suddenly she felt strong arms around her waist and froze. She felt the zing; its intensity penetrating to the visceral of her being. Did he feel it too? Shocked, she looked up into the stranger's eyes, and they too held surprise, confirming yes, he too felt it. Rayna sighed.

"I live a couple blocks away." She glanced down at her wet garb, and said, "I do appreciate your kindness." Rayna leaned back into his embrace, her ankle was a bit sore from her fall earlier. How he noticed was surprising to Rayna. "Let's get out of this storm," he said. Her heart accelerated at his closeness.

Rayna was too shocked to protest. Truth be told, she didn't

want to. It felt good being carried. This moment was surreal. She felt like a damsel in distress. She smiled, deciding to play the part. Besides, I'm never going to see my rescuer again, which is a pity, she thought. He smelled so good, like rain shower and pine. Rayna wrapped her arms around his neck and relaxed. The thought came to her that she seen had him somewhere before. What am I doing, Eric thought to himself.

This whole ridiculous scene felt right; to right. Eric had been on his way to the gym, and had decided to take a different route, when he saw Rayna jogging. He immediately recognized her. Either she was one heck of an actress, or she had totally forgotten their one meeting.

Eric couldn't understand why Rayna hadn't been hurrying home instead of jogging, as the storm clouds were gathering. He had started to drive away, but something staid him. Then she fell. He watched her. In the end, he wanted her. Rayna inhaled sharply. When they reached the sleek black Porsche, she knew there was no way she was going to damage something that beautiful, it just wasn't right.

"I'm going to get water all over your seat and mud on your floor. Look, maybe this is a bad idea. I'm already soaked through; I can just run the remaining blocks." Rayna was squirming in his arms. Eric started to protest, but his words were interrupted as lightning pierced the sky, followed by the loud sound of thunder. Rayna screamed, clinging tightly to her savior, all thoughts of protest forgotten.

Besides, the stranger looked like he could afford to have the Porsche cleaned. Thunder sounded again. God was not playing with her today. Rayna vowed to get to church early Sunday morning to repent for the things she has knowingly and unknowingly done.

He just laughed. Opening the passenger side door, he gently

placed Rayna inside. Rounding the car, he entered the driver's side, continuing to laugh. If a yawn was contagious maybe laughter was too, because Rayna soon found herself laughing with him. Seriously, one could not help but to laugh at the ridiculousness of the situation.

Her rescuer faced her and smiled. "Where to lady?" he asked. Sheila swallowed hard at his choice of words. "Murchison Road," she said. He just stared at her. Rayna wanted to break his hold but couldn't. Again came the feeling that she knew him from somewhere. Say something, she wanted to scream at him.

His hand shot out, moving a wet strand of hair from her eyes. Inhaling sharply, Rayna blinked twice, turning her attention to her folded hands. "Murchison Road it is then." Turning the key in the ignition, the car purred to life. The ride was bitter sweet for Rayna. The close confinement of the car enhanced sound and movement. It was still raining outside. Within a matter of minutes, the car had warmed up, defeating an earlier chill. Rayna leaned back.

Closing her eyes, she smiled. She felt peace settling over her. Her mystery man reminded her of the earth. His woodsy cologne, mixed with the rain, was a heady combination. "You know you support my theory that happiness can be gained in the rain." His voice was like a bucket of cold water. "Please don't stop smiling. A smile is a gift that very few people give or want to give, especially in the rain, or should I say in their pain?" he said. Rayna's eyes remained closed.

She wanted to know where this conversation was leading, so she remained still. "The rain is necessary at times. It's a cleanser. Have you ever noticed that after it rains, the world looks so refreshed? So revived?" He nodded his head. "Yes, the rain is a cleanser." Rayna finally understood. He'd witnessed her moment of releasing back there. She had released her pent up hurt in the rain, and yes, she felt refreshed. Was he called for a purpose in her life? She wanted to feel embarrassed but could not. Instead, she felt like she had gained a friend. She suddenly was overwhelmed with a need to confide in him.

"Right here," Rayna said, pointing to a moderate- sized two-story home when he turned onto Murchison Road. She was scared that her mystery man would or would not ask for her number. She anxiously waited. He pulled over to the curb, not cutting the engine off. Rayna unfastened her seatbelt and waited. Nothing. That was her clue. "Well, thanks for the ride," she said, opening the car door. He nodded. His car remained revved, indicating he was impatient to leave.

Rayna's heart plummeted with rejection and disappointment, which was stupid, considering she had just met him a second ago. "Thank you so much for rescuing me." She wanted him to do something, but didn't exactly know what. At the thought of never seeing him again, an unexpected sadness washed over her. She felt safe in his presence.

He stared. "I had better be going," she said. Say something, she thought in anguish. He nodded. Swallowing hard, Rayna exited the car; tears pricking her eyelids. Walking up her stairs, she could still hear his car engine running. Like her, it was running from this sudden attraction.

She was never an active participant in matters of the heart. She was the one sitting on the sidelines, watching the scenes play out with couples. Her life was more G rated; a 24-hour Nickelodeon marathon. Hands shaking, Rayna removed her keys from her pocket and opened the door, refusing to look back at the stranger. If she had spared a look, she would have seen him exiting his car, and purposely walking toward her. Eric was very close to Rayna when she finally managed to open her door. She hastily entered her abode; firmly closing the door behind her, closing both the world and him out. She never looked back.

That was the faithful day, he thought he'd walked away from her. He obviously left something behind because, try as hard as he could, he just couldn't get Rayna out of his mind. Eric found he wanted her; not just on a physical level; it was deeper than that. He wanted to know her likes and dislikes.

What made her smile? What made her angry? He examined those things, and was shocked to discover he wanted a landing place. For so long he felt as though he just was floating around in the world. Existing not living. With Rayna, he knew she was the anchor he needed. He wanted to know her.

There was no doubt about that. Yet, the timing was all wrong. He felt incomplete; his mother's murder was still out there somewhere. His gut was telling him, that he was close to finding her murderer, and soon. Until then, he couldn't possibly engage in a committed relationship. And who was that dude she was with at the restaurant? What annoyed him more was that he had to concede that they made a very striking couple; an updated Cliff and Claire Huxtable from 'The Cosby Show', he surmised.

He knew Rayna deserved peace and tranquility in her life and that those things were something he could never give her. He swallowed hard. What kind of highly trained professional was he, he wondered. One who had broken the golden rule, 'keep your emotions in check at all times, so that you can remain focused on the task in hand'.

He glanced at the file on his desk which contained more evidence regarding Mike's case. The pieces where slowly coming together he reassured himself and he would find the perpetrator responsible for that poor woman's death and the consequent havoc wrought in the life of his best friend.

Eric rose and crossed to the window. Looking out he could see the overcast blue green sky and observe the effect of its gloomy pallet on the surrounding area. There's going to be a storm on the way, he told himself. He was un-phased by the prospect; the drama of freak weather events, thunder and lightning included, had always fascinated him. A slow grin crossed his mouth as another thought made its way through his muddled mind.

"There seems to be a storm brewing on the inside, big brother." Came a familiar voice from behind him.

"I do believe that you're right, little brother. Good thing we came prepared." Another familiar voice added.

"As always, right on time," Eric whispered the words to himself and his grin became a broad smile. Pops had always warned them never to ignore the signs of a storm. He contemplated the personal similarities; often unpredictable, prone to fits of rage, tempestuous. Yep, that was him.

By nature, he was not a talkative man. Acquaintances would often mistake his reserve for arrogance. On the job, his counterparts admired his work ethic and consummate skills. In truth, he figured that no one really knew him for the man he was.

Out of the corner of his eye he glimpsed a couple of tall guys approaching him and he looked around just as they came to a standstill near where he stood. "What did I do to garner a visitation from the dynamic duo?" He asked the two brothers. The twins looked at each other smiling. "Uh, it's lunch time." They answered in unison. Smiling also, Eric looked at his watch and nodded.

Mike and Bryan led the way to his paper filled desk, and the three of them pulled up chairs and gathered around the medium sized square table. Bryan had done the honors this time; he lifted the lid of a large cooler box and started to hand out the parcels of wrapped food. Eric had been ready to make some sarcastic remark about the cooler box; but had second thoughts, upon smelling the appetizing aromas emanating from inside. Instead, he looked over at Mike and grinned.

"What's the fun, man?" Mike enquired.

"Nothing. Just wondering if you've gotten soft with the game," Eric stated distractedly, his mouth was seriously watering.

"Man, please. You two don't even know what I got in stored for you next week. Never under estimate the underdog." Mike stated.

Eric's eyes widened with mock surprise. "Oh, really? You see, the way I see it, your fixation with Sheila has neither improved nor sharpen your game, little man."

Bryan who was still busily placing food and drink items on the table quaffed aloud at the taunt.

Mike shot him a hard glance, "to the contrary, ol' man. Sheila has improved everything about me. My game included. In fact, she has taught me a new move that I'll show both you dudes, this Saturday. Called the hit'em hard movement." Mike began shuffling around in his seat animatedly.

Eric and Bryan looked at each other before breaking into spontaneous laughter, the contagious nature of which soon had mike joining them.

As they recovered their composure, Eric placed a hand briefly on Mike's shoulder, "you mean Sheila is going to let you play with the big dogs this weekend?" Eric made a sound like the cracking of a whip.

Mike stood briefly, shrugging his hand away, "what? You're tripping homey. My wife respects her man's space and don't mind my recreational activities, she knows I work hard and work even harder at pleasing her. We respect each other's space. Trust me; it's all good in the Montgomery household. So show some respect, playa."

Bryan smiled before biting into his sandwich, "I can see taking the family man road, and is a good road for you. Just as long as you aren't; having to ask permission every mile of the way."

"Believe you me, stifling each other is not what we do," Mike retorted.

"Good, because a bird was created to spread its wings," Eric chimed, he was glad of the pleasant distraction; a chance to push Rayna to the back of his mind for a while.

"Seriously though, look," Bryan's sober tones cut across the general spirit of hilarity. He looked deeply into the eyes of his brethrens. "Love has been given a bad rap, because it's often confused with lust. When a woman loves, she loves hard," he singled Eric out as he continued. "Take yourself, for example. You've got the money, house, and cars, but isn't there something missing?"

Eric wiped his mouth, balled up his napkin and threw it into the trash can. Smiling smugly at the twins, when it landed neatly inside. "Man, Bryan, I don't want to hear about women and their hearts. It's too complicated. Anyways, what about a man and his heart? And weddings? Why do they have to be about the woman? Weddings are biased. I am staying away from them."

Bryan smiled lopsidedly as if trying to conceal a secret, "I tell you the truth and then I am going to move on. Love is risky. It's downright scary because you have to open yourself up to another person. This takes trust." He looked at both men. "I learned to trust my wife after we were married, not before. This made for a rocky experience for us. Thank God, for patience and counselling from Pops." Mike and Eric exchanged a brief look, this was the first time, both men had heard about this.

Bryan continued on. "I knew that I loved her with everything inside of me. I just never felt I was good enough for her. There was always this small fear that she would wake up and tell me that she no longer loved me. That she deserved better. That's why I worked as hard as I did when I was in real estate. I knew I was chosen to preach the gospel but I wanted to please her first. Valerie knew something wasn't right.

One night she had this incredible dinner set up for the both of us. And we began to talk in the language of love. I listened to every word she said with my mind and heart. She thought she was holding me back, and she was willing to leave me so I could be the man I wanted to be. I confessed that I wasn't happy with my career choice. And, I will never forget what the love of my life did next."

"Yeah?" Eric urged him on.

"She slapped me!"

Both men looked at Bryan before laughing boisterously. Yes, that was something, Valeria would do. They laughed even harder still when he began rubbing his left cheek in recollection.

"She told me that all that time, I had her believing she was the problem, and it was me all along." Bryan grinned lopsidedly. He also recalled how the night ended, and their future began from that day on. He was certainly a blessed man. Now, so were Mike and Sheila. Next was Eric, he knew this to be true.

He had visions both he and Eric had them since they were toddlers. They can see things, and right now, Bryan clearly saw Rayna in Eric's life. He wouldn't tell Eric this of course. Bryan knew the future didn't need in influence from him. What's God has planned for the life of people, can't be stopped. It may be blocked at times, but never stopped.

The conversation went on, cutting back a forth between topics, views and witticisms. Eric enjoyed their company enormously but at some point during the course of these light hearted exchanges, he distinctly detected that Mike seemed to have disengaged.

"Hey, Mike, you're not thinking about Shelia, again, are you?" He leaned across and gently punched the man's arm.

"Nah," Mike responded unconvincingly.

"Mike?" Eric prompted, sensing that he was onto something that he was keen to tease out.

Mike sat in silence for a moment or two, "not thinking about

Sheila." He said quietly. Truthfully, he was thinking of Sheila and his ex-wife and their unborn child. This NWO, had their lives in limbo. Mike constantly lived in fear that someone was going to leap out of the shadows and try to take Sheila from him again.

He truly believed he couldn't survive that kind of heartbreak ever again. He just couldn't. Mike was glad for the extra eyes and protection from his twin brother and Eric. Yet still, he wanted closure for him and his family. If anyone was deserving of authentic happiness it was his family. Mike sighed heavily.

Bryan seemed to pick up on the cue; he looked across at Eric as if to suggest something, "Leave it, man." He said instead.

This intrigued Eric further, "not Sheila? Then what?" He asked in all innocence, knowing the answer as soon as the words had left his mouth. "Oh. I see." He could have kicked himself for pushing it. Clearly the man had been thinking about his former wife, Marie. He caught Mike's questioning eyes staring at him now, seeking any answers Eric had to give.

"Tell me," Mike urged Eric.

Eric looked at Bryan who nodded his head in slow affirmation.

"Actually, there has been a bit of a break through," he paused to check Mike's reaction, and to catch Bryan's eye before continuing. "I don't think what happened that night was an accident, I'm almost convinced the two of you were attacked."

Mike and Bryan glanced at each other and nodded their heads simultaneously as if communicating via telepathy. In the past, Eric had referred to the brother's ability to exchange information in this way as a 'twin thing'.

"There is an organization or cult that has headquarters set up around the World. Who believe in a New World Order, by which they mean purification of this world?"

"I don't understand," Bryan shook his head in confusion.

"What are you saying? That we have a modern day Hitler on

our hands?" Mike sounded incredulous.

Eric leaned back into his chair and looked out his office window, the police station was almost empty due to the lunch hour; his office door stood ajar. He scanned the canteen to make sure none of his colleagues could overhear him. The room was quiet; the big return from lunchtime rush, hadn't started yet. "My investigations and undercover work have led me to conclude that these people genuinely exist. That they certainly believe they are the true world leaders. And, that they have power, influence and ample resources."

Bryan's eyes hardened, "surely, something as big as this couldn't have gone undetected up until now? Has it been hidden, who's been keeping us in the dark?"

"People in high places have been aiding their cause, little brother."

Mike leaned forward, "who exactly? Who?"

Eric shrugged. "Doctors, lawyers, cops. And, you guessed it, politicians, too. There are many and varied, my brothers." Eric looked each man squarely in the eyes emphasizing the seriousness of the situation. "We are up against something huge, something so evil it almost seems unstoppable. It's hard to know who to trust, it's like one huge game of deceit. Bryan, you remember the stake out that went awry last year?"

Bryan was quick to respond. "The one that almost landed your partner, Levitz, in intensive care?"

"Yeah, that one. That night he was antsy, kept glancing at his watch and rubbing the cross around his neck. He asked me if God hears the cries of a sinner."

"There's nothing odd about that question," Bryan asserted.

"No there isn't," Eric agreed. "Only Levitz is supposed to be a devout Christian."

Bryan's pending question was cut short as Eric held up the

palm of one hand and continued, "Before you go into your, all have fallen short of the glory, spiel. I echoed those same words to Levitz, myself. Then he really did become agitated, began ranting about, the movement, and how he was in too deep and couldn't get out. That the Apocalypse was coming. The Remnant was the chosen ones.

They would be the ones to help save the world from this growing evil." Eric looked at the twins. "Levitz was a rookie; it was his first stakeout, so quite naturally I assumed he was chatting due to nerves. Next thing I know, our perp comes out of the building, recognizes us instantly and flees. We pursue, the perp pulls his weapon and Levitz takes a bullet in the stomach. It was a decision between Levitz and the perp."

"You chose Levitz," Bryan filled in the gap.

"I'd chosen Levitz. The punk got away," Eric nodded before casting a weary glance in Mike's direction.

"You mean there's some freak organization out there masquerading as representatives of the church, with the belief that they are the true leaders of the world?" Mike who had been sitting and absorbing in silence sounded totally unconvinced.

"I know what you're thinking, man," Eric addressed him directly. "The church is supposed to be a place of refuge and safety, so why would it be trying to hurt and kill good people, people like yourself and Marie."

Mike swallowed hard, choking back the hurt of bitter past emotional pain.

"I went to see Monica at the safe house yesterday," Eric was referring to the key witness in the NWO case, who also happened to be Sheila's half-sister. Sheila was shocked by the discovery just a few short months ago, the startling revelation was confirmed before her father was brutally murder by one of the members of the NWO.

"How are she and the baby doing?" Mike inquired of his

sister-in-law and niece.

"They're adjusting, considering the unusual circumstances. Hopefully, once we've identified the leader of this sick group, they'll be able to live some sort of normal life again."

"I don't think they will ever consider themselves normal again," Mike corrected in earnest.

All three men grew silent, each deep in their own thoughts. "I agree. But, they are trying, I give them that much. I also will give you my word that I will find those who are responsible for Marie's death and make them pay." Eric didn't blink an eye.

Bryan started to say something; one look from Eric stopped all protests. He simply nodded. Eric looked at Mike and Bryan. "Also, I think that the NWO maybe somehow connected." As he expected Mike and Bryan was stunned. Then the twin's faces simultaneously growing stormy. All three men agreed to meet each other on the court Saturday for their Basketball game.

Eric's mind once again returned to Rayna. Shaking his head, he decided to go do some investigative work outside. Suddenly the room had become too confining for him. Exiting the station Eric inhaled the fresh air, once again grateful to see another day. He never took daily living for granted. Getting into his unmarked company car, Eric headed down town, determined to exercise Rayna out of his mind. It worked for ten minutes.

Chapter 8

"Would you stop staring at me," Rayna commanded, sighing as she placed her tea cup down with more force than she had intended.

Sheila tilted her head to the side, studying her best friend. "There is something different about you, Rayna." Sheila swept her hand up and down in Rayna's direction. "I mean you are more ebullient than your normal self. And, that right there is scary. Really, how much cheerfulness can a person take?" She gave Rayna a sideways glance, "so spill it."

I want to know what is fuelling this happy streak of yours. Matter of fact, lately you've been quite reserved with information." Sheila sliced into the fillet of baked salmon on her place and consumed a mouthful eagerly. "My goodness, I can never tire of eating here. This is the best salmon, ever."

"It's a good thing you're married, because eating like that will get you nowhere with the men," Rayna remarked sarcastically.

Sheila devoured another fork full. "I can't help it. Seriously, this salmon is literally melting in my mouth, Rayna." Sheila held her folk aloft and waved it as if to show her delight. "And don't try to distract me; I want to know what's going on with you."

Rayna arched one brow, and sipped gingerly from her coffee cup. "There is nothing going on with me," she shrugged modestly. "Well, nothing out of the norm that is," she placed her cup back on its coaster and leaned in. "Although, I am excited about this particular case I'm working on, I have a feeling this will be the one that will make me partner. Oh, and Philip and I are doing wonderful and…"

"Hold on. You and Philip are still dating?" Sheila looked at her with knowing eyes.

Rayna could never hide anything from her friend. She prepared herself for the onslaught that she sensed was about to come her way. She didn't want to hear about how she and Philip were total opposites, or how they were both too busy for it to work, or how they were bound to fail to make time for one another. Though she had never admitted it to Sheila, she couldn't deny that the fact that they had so little time to spare for one another really irked her. She would much rather there was more time available outside of her hectic schedule. Ultimately, she wanted to be able to spend quality time with her partner, just as Sheila and Mike did.

Mike, she felt, was sensitive to Sheila's needs and wants. When she talked, his focus was 100 percent on her. This train of thought always led in the same direction, she realized - only now she'd realized it, it was a little too late. Sure enough she found herself thinking about Eric, unfortunately.

She reiterated to herself, Eric doesn't want you and you just have to get over him. Her mind was made up, she would enjoy her newfound relationship with Phil, and all thoughts of Eric would be buried. Whether her heart was on the same page however, was another matter.

Rayna felt like she was walking on pins and needles because they were at Eric's restaurant again. She hadn't wanted to come here for obvious reasons but her efforts to dine elsewhere proved null and void. Sheila was like a dog drawn to a bone; once she latched on to something, there was no letting go. She had told Rayna that she'd heard rave reviews about the place and the genuine entrepreneurial spirit of its owners, who had garnered a certain amount of local publicity for their venture. After that, she was determined to come and see for herself what all the hype was about.

"I'm sorry I'm late," the newcomer, a pretty young woman

caught their attention as she arrived at their table. "My last appointment ran a little longer than I anticipated."

Sheila stood enthusiastically and gave the woman a hug, "Maya, you made it! We'd just started, so not to worry. I received your message for us to go ahead and order as you didn't know if you'd make it or not." Sheila cast a hesitant glance in Rayna's direction as she returned to her seat.

"For a moment there, I thought I wouldn't but for some reason I felt a strong need to make this luncheon," Maya looked at Rayna and smiled.

"Maya, let me introduce you to my dearest friend in the whole world. Rayna meet Maya Stone. Maya meet Rayna Peterson." Sheila smiled at both ladies as if that explained everything.

"I am pleased to finally meet you, Rayna. I've heard only good things about you."

Rayna smiled in Maya's direction, some of her displeasure at having a stranger invited to their meeting was evaporating. Maya's smile was contagious.

"Sheila's praise of me does not always deserve, I do have my ugly moments, trust me. Shelia hasn't mentioned you before, Maya, now that is unusual." Sheila's only response was to take another bite of her salmon.

Maya caught sight of the food on their plates, "Yummy, your meals look divine. I think I'll have a salad from the bar for time's sake. Excuse me ladies." Maya walked gracefully towards the salad bar. She was statuesque and had long bountiful hair. Rayna notice the attention she attracted from other diners and the way in which she seemed oblivious to it all.

"Rayna, I know what you're thinking, so let me allay your feelings now. Maya is a life coach. She just joined our What-a-Lady meeting, and she is fierce. She's counselled countless women all over the world, helping them to reconnect with life and themselves." Sheila drew closer to her friend. "She's not married but was once engaged. She was in an abusive relationship."

Rayna's eyes widened in alarm.

"It wasn't physical abuse. It was hard core verbal." Sheila stated shaking her head.

"Abuse is abuse, Sheila. It doesn't matter what form it comes in," Rayna affirmed, all the time watching Maya as she continued to make her choices over at the salad bar. She wore a two-piece plum colored pant suit. It was professional attire, yet on her, it looked runway. Maya's jewelry looked expensive; small diamond studs and a gold cross necklace.

She looked so confident and at ease with herself. Rayna was baffled. Why would men treat a treasure like that, as trash? Granted, she didn't really know Maya but she did regard herself a good judge of character. She always felt that if you paid close enough attention to a person, you could see their true personality - living a lie 24 hours a day was hard to do.

"I agree with you my dear friend. Some people however, think abuse is only what happens when a man or woman lay hands on one another, and I'm not talking about in prayer, either." Rayna nodded in agreement. "For some reason, I was instinctively drawn to Maya. She has a lovely spirit, and she's pretty new in town and in need of some friends." Sheila sat back as if pleased to get back to eating the salmon.

Rayna could sense that Sheila was hiding something from her but thought better of pressing her about it. All their lives it seemed as though she'd been trying to protect Rayna from anything she considered a threat to her. When they'd been at college together, Shelia had gone out of her way to watch out for her, and to ensure she kept herself safe from harm.

"I'm still curious as to why you didn't tell me."

"Well for one, when I invited her today, I didn't think she'd actually make it. She's a very successful coach and is usually busy, and secondly I knew you'd think I was up to something." Sheila looked knowingly at her friend, a semi-sincere look on her face.

Maya had returned to the table, her plate filled with salad and fresh fruit. Shelia made space for her to sit down.

"So Sheila tells me you're a life coach?" Rayna started their group conversation.

Maya poured sugar into her tea, stirring it she smiled, "Since I was a little girl, I've always known that I wanted to help people. I knew I couldn't be a Doctor; I didn't have the fortitude to cut on people. I knew I wouldn't be a Lawyer, either. An unethical career. So, I re-evaluated my skills. I felt I was good at listening and offering advice. I'm quite caring." Maya beamed, "a friend of mine suggested I become a life coach. I loved the sound of that, so, I pursued my BA and Master's Degrees in Psychology, and then joined the International Association of Coaching. The rest, as they say, is history.

Sheila sipped from her glass, "You are going to love our What-a-Lady group."

"I'm sure that I am. Growing up I didn't have many friends. I've always wanted to be a part of a sisterhood."

Sheila addressed Rayna, "speaking of girl talk, Maya will be coming along to the group when we next meet. We've added another chapter to our book of healing, entitled, 'Call Me Victorious'. By the way, we're still waiting for your contribution, Rayna." Sheila gently reminded Rayna. Rayna nodded.

Maya's eyes widen with excitement, "I can't wait to meet with the ladies. My brief experience with some of them had a big impact on me. Made me feel renewed. Sometimes it's great to be able to share experiences with people like yourself."

Sheila inched closer to Maya, briefly hugging her, "there's strength in numbers. Some of those women have been through hell like you could never imagine. Yet they still manage to live and not only exist in the world."

"That is exactly what I was doing," Maya looked at Rayna and then Sheila, a faint smile gracing her lips. "Only, I hadn't realized it at the time."

"The hardest part is letting go. I tell the ladies this at the center, all the time. D'you know it takes at least seven episodes of abuse before an abused person decides to leave the abuser? They are afraid of the unknown, starting over again, or they've been brained washed so bad into thinking they are worthless and that no one could ever love them," Sheila declared passionately.

"I admire your hard work and the dedication, Sheila. You're like a clarion call in this neighborhood. You even got the Mayor involved." Maya popped a baby tomato into her mouth, chewed briefly and then emitted a radiant smile, which lit up her whole face.

Sheila again wondered why some men chose to abuse, and not cherish, their partners - gifts from God, she thought.

Sheila shrugged, "I have to confess, I am blessed. It was hard going at first. At times the pace is still slow, dealing with red tape, but it's better to be safe than sorry. I have countless women's life on the line."

Rayna nodded reflecting on Shelia's support group. She'd been a member for over three months now. She'd been broken when she joined but hearing the powerful stories of other women, she had discovered that she could overcome her struggles with self-doubt and feelings of rejection. The group had never rushed her or any of her fellow members.

The choice to share your testimony was always your own. Rayna was beginning to feel that her time to share was close. She thought about how she had almost lost her life those few months ago and shuddered. To say that she would never be the same was not an understatement; it was the stone cold truth. She used to see the world through rose tinted lenses but now, those were the days of old. The new day featured a less gullible, stronger woman.

Looking around the restaurant, Sheila felt invigorated by the bustle of the place. There were people from all walks of live enjoying good food and company. She noticed that people seemed cheerful and contented, for the most part, but she also knew that they couldn't all be feeling that way.

Casting illusions, she thought, people project illusions of their lives on the world. She should know because she had done exactly that herself for years. Until, she met Mike. Her heart leapt at the thought of her husband. He was her rock and saving grace. She never thought she would love or be loved; growing up in a foster home, losing her mother in tragic, violent circumstances, had left her feeling lost and incapable of expressing love.

She'd always known that true love existed but she couldn't envisage it visiting her door. Never in a million years had she thought a man like her husband would fall in love and marry a woman like her. He was handsome and kind, and considerate. She shivered at the thought of his intense dark eyes, full lips and pecan colored skin. Sheila was roused from her daydreaming by the sound of Rayna's voice. She had obviously been trying to say something to her.

Rayna now looked wounded as she spoke, "would you please give me your undivided attention for just a couple of hours? Sheesh." She groaned and slanted her head to emphasis her playful plca. She seemed to observe her friend for a minute and then changed her tone of voice, "you, know, from the way you're eating I wouldn't be surprised at all if you were pregnant."

Sheila smirked, "perhaps I'm just in love. It found me and I know it'll find you one of these fine days."

Narrowing her eyes suspiciously, Rayna gave Sheila a long look. She would never in a million years admit how much she wanted Sheila's words to be true. She could count her past relationships on one hand and they had hardly been stellar affairs. Yes, she was blessed with good looks but this was also her

Achilles heel. It seemed she was forever fighting the stigma of beauty and no brains. "I'm not entirely convinced by that. Is there something you're not telling me? Because, if there is, you're violating code number 245 in the best friend handbook."

"What handbook? There's no such thing," Sheila countered.

"Besties are not to withhold pertinent life changing info from each other," Rayna continued on as if she'd never been interrupted.

Sheila smiled but she sensed some genuine concern behind the light hearted comment. "Relax. What, are you afraid I'm trying to hook you up with someone? Well, I'm not but come to think of it, it isn't a bad idea." Sheila raised her hand cutting off whatever Rayna was about to say. "Cameron has expressed a solid interest in you for years now," Shelia sighed and leaned back in her chair. "I know I've mentioned it before, but it's not like I'm asking you to marry the guy, just go out on one date with him. In any event, it'll get you out of the house; enjoy a nice meal, some pleasant company."

"Well lookey here, is that the time. I hate to eat and run but I promised Philip I'd bring him lunch today," Rayna pushed he plate aside and rose suddenly. "Maya, it was a pleasure to meet you, and looking forward to seeing you at the meeting."

"We're not done, Rayna," Sheila's tone was only half serious.

Rayna continued to gather her things, "yes we are. Tootles." She placed her designer shades on and waved goodbye to the two women as she made her swift exit.

Sheila caught a glimpse of what she felt was an annoyed look on Maya's face as her friend left.

Maya took a sip of her tea, pausing for a moment, "I like her." She said smilingly.

Sheila reconsidered; maybe she'd just imagined it. She looked at Maya, affected a comical look of strain on her face, "so do I...sometimes."

* * *

Rayna had reached the door of the restaurant and overheard a man grumbling, followed by some loud noises coming from the reception area.

"You imbecile. Your clumsiness is quite remarkable."

Rayna looked over at the chaos. A large irate man had collided with one of the waitresses and was trying to wipe something off his shirt, whilst demeaning the apologetic looking member of staff.

"I have dined at the finest of eateries, and never have I encountered such an atrocious display of service. This is simply unacceptable."

Rayna was discomforted by the scene and felt sorry for the poor waitress as she tried to put things right and apologize. Just then, the man turned and she caught a glimpse of the anger and hatred in his eyes. What a weirdo, she thought, as she pushed open the door and made her exit.

Back at the table, Maya and Sheila were oblivious to the brief commotion, "…I understand. By the way, I wanted to express my appreciation for inviting me to the group, a chance to be amongst some like-minded women."

Sheila raised her glass, "cheers to auspicious beginnings."

Maya tilted her cup in reciprocation before placing it back on the table, "can I tell you something that might seem a little off the wall?"

"Sure, why not."

Maya looked around the restaurant and lowered her voice, "I am almost embarrassed to say, but I feel comfortable around you. As I was saying earlier, my ur…relationship with Larry…"

"Abusive," Shelia was firm and yet assumed a comforting

tone. "It was an abusive relationship, Maya."

Maya nodded her acknowledgement, "well, it lasted about two years. Two years two long. When I first met him...Larry. He knew all the right words to say. Those sweet things that make a woman feel good about herself. I must have been lonely or something, because at the time, I took it all in. I mean, there's only so much you can do on your own, living the single life, but ultimately, I felt I was missing something."

Maya surveyed her surrounds carefully again before continuing. "Well, it wasn't long before we moved in together, and shortly thereafter he changed. He started demanding that we take our relationship to another level," Maya paused to sip her tea.

"You mean he wanted to have sexual relations?" Shelia asked.

Maya looked embarrassed, "yes. I wasn't ready for that. At first, he seemed cool with it but his behavior started changing towards me. He was aloof and moody, and the compliments stopped. I knew I was losing him, and yet I couldn't bring myself to sleep with him. The verbal abuse began around that time. I was too skinny.

No one would ever want a woman like me. The way I walked and talk was disgusting, and that I should be glad a man like him was even interested in someone like me..." Maya struggled to control her emotions as a tear formed in her eye and ran down her cheek.

Sheila was quick to offer her a napkin, "Maya, I know this is painful for you. Can I ask how it eventually ended?"

Maya eyes became distant. "One night Larry came home drunk. I will never forget that night as long as I live. It was late, and in a way, I guess I'd already made up my mind that I was going to leave him but that didn't save me from the shock I experienced. He'd brought another woman home; she was drunk too, of course. He was blatantly disrespectful, started kissing and fondling her, right in my face, right in our home. That's when I snapped." Maya looked at Shelia directly, "I'd decided I didn't want to carry all that negative energy anymore. I'd been bottling it up and I just let him have it, began yelling and shouting. I think I even punched the girl he was with. Think I broke her nose, I found out later.

He threw me on the floor, called me some unrepeatable names, even tried to choke me at one point…" She looked vulnerable and on the verge of tears again. "It…was…terrible. I saw my life past before me. I couldn't breathe, couldn't scream. Just when I thought I was going to pass out, he let me go. I can still hear his taunting laughter and his departing words."

The look of understanding on Sheila's face encouraged Maya to go on.

"He said I'd never amount to anything. No one wants trash like you, he told me, not even your parents." Maya's voice sounded distant as said relived the words.

Sheila nodded sympathetically, and touched Maya's hand as a sign of solidarity and support. She still found it hard to believe how the world could harbor so much evil or people who were so unhappy. "That monster didn't deserve the time you gifted him."

"Well, I don't know where he is now, and I don't care anymore. I'm just glad that he's no longer my problem. I've found myself again, and I'll never let me go."

"I'll drink to that," Sheila lightened the mood, raising her glass of water once more.

"So will I," Maya picked up her cup and touched it to Sheila's. "So will I."

* * *

Sometime later that day, Rayna was still feeling the negative after effects resulting from the evil look, the arrogant man at the restaurant had given her. She thought about calling Phil to come meet her but as she reached for her cell phone, she changed her mind; she felt like an idiot. What would she tell him? That some man had given her a hard stare and badly shaken her up, how would that have sounded?

She tried to distract herself by thinking back on Sheila's comments of earlier.

'Perhaps I'm just in love. It found me and I know it'll find you one of these fine days.'

Her dear friend truly wanted the best for her and that was a comforting thought. At the same time she couldn't get over the feeling that Sheila was hiding something from her, although she knew it would do no good to press her into revealing what it was. It seemed all their lives Sheila had been trying to protect her, from anything she considered a threat.

Back in their college days, they'd both joined the track and field team and entered trials for the 800 meters final. Sheila was a great athlete and with her amazing sprinting ability had easily made the cut. She, on the other hand, had been more of an all-rounder, very capable at middle distances but her place in the team was far from assured.

There had been a lot of hard work, requiring both mental and physical stamina to make the grade. In the end it had come down to a competition between her and another girl. She tried to recall her challenger's name – she could remember the girl been incredibly determined to gain a position. Then it came to her, Veronica Hightower. Veronica was a petite Latina, with long flowing raven hair which she tended to keep pinned up.

When not pinned, the heavy mass fell in silky waves down her back and the girls on the track team had nick named her 'Speedy'. They were both excellent runners but only one could get the last remaining place.

Their coach, Donahue, had given the two of them his standard, 'we are a team' speech, implying that no one could really be a loser but everyone had known he was just trying to soften the blow for the girl who did eventually lose out. On the day of the deciding race between her and Veronica, the other team members had stood on the side-lines, privately rooting for their favored runner. Coach Donahue had blown his whistle and she had taken off, acutely aware that Speedy was a solid contender.

She had run faultlessly, poetry-in-motion, she recalled, as she had tried to use everything she'd learned, and apply every technique she knew to get ahead. As they'd approached the final bend, she'd felt as if she was losing ground and felt as if she had very little more to give but it was then that Shelia's excited yells and loud encouraging chants had picked her up. As she'd neared the finish line - Veronica still very much in contention - she'd felt as though her breath was trapped in her throat.

For a moment, she felt she might pass out. Still, she found another burst of energy and ducked at the line, stumbling as she crossed. The team members had screamed in victory and she realized she had won. The girls ran over to Rayna and lifted her up onto their shoulders cheering and applauding. Sheila had kept her faith in her girl and that steadfast belief had carried her over the line or that's what it had felt like.

A few hours later, Rayna's mind had once again returned to the brief harrowing incident of earlier, at the restaurant. She was still unable to completely shake it off. The event lingered in her mind and into the night. As she lay in her bed; she had a strong urge to call Eric, of all people. The desire was so strong it almost seemed like a compulsion. "Stop it," she muttered. As she turned over she reached for her well-worn Bible and read the familiar passage, Psalms 23. This made her feel a little better, and she even managed a little smile before she turned off the lamp and settled into a peaceful sleep.

* * *

Philip felt a genuine sense of interruption at the sound of the firm repetitive knock on his office door. As it swung open, he looked up and was surprised to see a tall well-built man stepping in and closing the door firmly behind him.

"I hate to interrupt you, it's obvious you're busy, but, after I didn't get a reply I thought I'd just better come on in," the man explained with a shrug. "Your secretary wasn't at the front desk, so I came on back. I'm Detective Eric Miller. I need to ask you some question concerning a case I am working on."

Philip heard the words but was also acutely aware of the baritone voice that delivered them. Philip, felt as though he met him before. He stood up instinctively and reached out a hand in greeting, gesturing for Eric to sit down.

Without making it obvious, Eric took in the layout and decor of the modest room; peach color walls, dark wooden desk, couple of book shelves, black leather sofa. Reassuringly for Eric, there was some clutter but generally the place was neat and tidy. He caught the faint strains of classical jazz music coming from speakers that he couldn't see. It was tasteful, he thought.

Philip, glanced passed Eric. "Kayla, my secretary must be in the storage room, please make yourself comfortable."

Eric sat on the sofa, which was firmer than he'd been expecting. He noticed Philip's array of certificates lined up on one wall. A man with an education, he noted.

"I understand you recently carried out surgery on a young woman who may have a connection to one of our cases."

Philip breathed out audibly. What's all this about, he was thinking, as he looked at the well-dressed cop sitting upright on his expensive sofa. "That's interesting," he said, sounding deliberately disinterested. "I'm quite busy, with all due respect, Detective, as I'm sure you are." He noticed that Eric was watching him intently and started to form the impression that there was more to this than the fact that it simply involved one of his patients. Philip tried to place the man's name as he felt he'd definitely seen him before.

Eric eventually spoke, "the patient was a young girl who you operated on very recently. Bit of a miraculous recovery job, by all accounts apparently." He waited for the recognition in Philip's eyes.

"Yes. That poor girl, she could have died, almost did die on the operating table…"

"But, you brought her back to life?" Eric finished the sentence sounding matter of fact.

Philip shook his head, "it's a miracle she's alive today." He paused, uncertain for a moment what to say next before recovering, "I am afraid she's in a coma in ICU, not much help to you at the moment."

Eric had already established that the girl was under police protection. "I understand, I'll try not to inconvenience you too much. You see, she's currently under our radar as a possible witness in the case of an extreme religious cult. They call themselves The New World Order." Eric waited, scanning Philip's reaction for any sign of acknowledgement.

Philip's eyes widened with excitement and interest. Like everyone else, he'd heard of the case on the news.

"We're inclined to believe that your Jane Doe is on some kind of NWO hit list."

Philip looked out of the large window situated to the left of his desk as though to remove himself from the confines of his office.

"The woman's landlord discovered her on the verge of death at her apartment. After calling for an ambulance, he rang the police as he suspected it was more than just an accident."

"The responding officers found a small journal amongst her possessions. It has some cryptic notation scrawled inside, and that was the link to the NWO. We had a specialist linguistic analyst decipher the book, and as a result we've reason to believe she's still in danger."

Philip looked unconvinced, "that's hard to believe. Do you think the whole protection thing is necessary, Detective Miller? We try to maintain a sense of calm and stability here at Saint Andrews, so the prospect of armed cops running around the place is hardly conducive. Besides, she's in a coma."

Eric stirred but remained silent.

"That particular operation has to be one of the most complicated I've performed. I'm certainly praying for the best, but only God knows when she may awake up. People can stay in that condition for years. Is that even your intention Detective, to guard her for as long as it takes?"

"Like you Doctor Stephens, we're praying, and hoping for the best," Eric confessed. "We don't want to cause any additional difficulty to you, your staff or your facility. It's just about protecting a potential victim, keeping her safe from these crazies."

Philip stared out of the window as Eric talked, and Eric took the opportunity to look him over. This was the man who'd captured the attention of Rayna, well, he could just about understand why. Philip appeared to be stable, respectable and compassionate; the kind of man Rayna deserved and would feel safe with.

"I do understand," Philip looked at him sincerely, "and we'll be happy to cooperate, if that's the best thing for our patient, then it's the best thing for us all."

"Thanks, Doctor Stephens," Eric was genuinely impressed by the man's caring attitude towards his patients. He Rose to leave.

"By the way, Detective, I have the distinct sense that I know you from somewhere."

"Yes, that is likely. You see, the other evening, possibly the very day you operated on Ms. Jane Doe, I saw you in the Heart and Soul restaurant."

Philip looked relieved, as though a missing piece had finally fallen into place, "ah, the Heart and Soul, that's it. That's it. Great food, great…"

"Atmosphere," Eric filled in, "yeah, I know."

Philip looked sharply at Eric. Certain that he felt heated undercurrents. "Yes, great atmosphere." Philip sat back down indicating their meeting was officially over. Eric smiled trying to intimidate. Philip nodded his head, leaned back and crossed his legs. "Detective Miller, I will keep all you've said into consideration. But would like to serve as a reminder, that I will always do what's in the best interest of the patient."

Eric nodded his head before exiting. He would get nothing else from Dr. Stephens this day.

Chapter 9

It was the second Sunday of the month. That meant Pops Montgomery would be preaching today. Pop Montgomery semi-retired from preaching last year, passing on the Pastor ship to his son, Bryan. Rayna was glad she decided to come to church earlier than normal. The Sanctuary was utterly packed. The atmosphere was thick with excitement for several reasons. One there was a special musical guest that would be ministering today.

Amber Bullock was 2011 winner of the BET reality show, Sunday best. The church was beatific to look upon. In the rain or sunshine, its beauty never went unnoticed. It was nestled in downtown Atlanta. It was set a ways off from the highway, giving it a suburban feel. The landscape was utterly gorgeous. Five large maple trees stood erect. Flowers of all kind were in full bloom, their sweet scents often wafting in the wind.

Deliverance Missionary Hope Church now held 1200 members strong, and it continues to grow. Its missionary ministry was Rayna's favorite auxiliary. Rayna was an active member of the church; serving as legal advisor, and was a member of the Women's Board and Missionary Board. She loved visiting the prisons, sharing the gospel. She never pressed her belief on anyone, she merely shared the joy and experience she had on her faith walk. She was from Detroit, Michigan; her mother did what she could to raise her. She worked several jobs, as a single child, Rayna was often lonely and had no one to talk to growing up.

Her mother instilled in her the importance of getting of going to school and getting a good job. Rayna not only finished college, graduating magna cum laude, she went on to obtain her law degree. Now she was a practicing Attorney at Law for Hudson, Fist and Hudson. On the outside it looked as though she had it all together.

There was something missing, she didn't know what it was. Well until last year, she didn't. Until that fateful day, when she decided to go jogging and the rain came out of nowhere, she fell trying to run home; in the sudden downpour. It was then Eric came out of nowhere, assisting her. To her chagrin, she mistook him for a thief. Eric shrugged the offense off and merely explained her only wanted to assist her home.

Reluctantly, she allowed him to drive her the short distance to her home. The ride was magnetic, it was like some invisible force had tied them together, and the connection was just that powerful in the car. Alas, the fantasy bubble was popped, when Eric stated aloud, how he wasn't interested in a relationship. Rayna was hurt and felt rejected.

Which again, made no sense, she didn't know him. But, the pull. The conversation they shared, it was as if they met somewhere before, as if they knew each other. Rayna lifted her chin and agreed, stated she too wasn't interested in a relationship, as her schedule didn't permit her to do so.

Rayna was dressed in an elegant 2 piece cream color dress and jacket set. The natural waist dress side panels were decorated with a black intricate geometric design. On her head was a Slight asymmetrical tilted black had with metallic stud band trimmings on the edges. She was fierce and she knew it. But it wasn't about fashion today.

Today was about being thankful of seeing another day. Rayna was also going to pray a prayer of strong protection for her family and friends as of late she had been feeling a deep sense of foreboding, she had also been experiencing restless sleep. It was as if something wholly evil was sleeping restlessly in the dark, stirring patiently waiting it's time to rise up.

Rayna looked around the familiar edifice and was immediately comforted. "Greetings sister, Rayna. It's good to see you on this fine Sunday morning." Rayna smiled at the familiar voice. She turned in looked into the wizen eyes of one of eldest Mothers of the church.

"Good morning, Mother Hattie." Rayna briefly embraced the octogenarian in greeting. I got the impress this is going to quite a unique service today." Rayna nodded her head in agreement. "Don't want to linger too long. Service is about to begin. You go on in, baby." "Aren't you going in? We could sit together?" Rayna asked.

"Um, not just yet." Mother Hattie looked over her shoulder. "I am waiting for someone. Once they arrive, I can take my seat." Rayna smiled. "OK. I will try to save you a seat, then."

"Yes, baby. Keep a place open. Rayna frowned slightly at her choice of words. Opting not to say anything, she simply nodded and entered to sanctuary. All the Montgomery clan were in the reserved seating. Rayna was led to the third aisle where two seats remained. Settling into her seat she suddenly felt as though she was being watched. Refusing to allow the eerie sensation to stop her praise of thanksgiving she joined in with praise and worship.

* * *

Corbin followed the Triune from afar, hiding in the shadows. He was very cautious not to alert the deadly three of his presence. They had a hit on Drakus, due his failure in capturing their last target. The Triune was looking for the true bride of the organization. The true breeder with true blood that was birth forth a new generation. All the others were her attendees, also breeders.

It was late in the evening, the sun had long ago set. Corbin was amazed at how they were able to walk amongst so many people and no one paid them too much attention. They hurriedly moved out of the three way or pretended not to notice them. The three looked out of place, medieval in fact. Like druids.

They wore long black robes, walking with their heads down. This was evidence of the world we live in Corbin thought. No one cared anymore. Evil was taking place in their backyard and no one noticed. He shook his head in the negative. No. They chose not to notice.

The Triune stopped in front of what looked like an abandoned warehouse. He leaned against the wall and waited. The tallest of the three was talking into a mouth piece. He was Dimitri their leader. He was the chosen one for the true bride of Zion. One of them suddenly looked around as if sensing something. He was Loren. He was the evil in its pure form. Loren was ruthless, no mercy was in him.

The third one looked at him in question. He was Stone. Rightfully named, as he had a heart of stone. He could look you direct in the eye and kill and lie. There was not one ounce of mercy in him. If he went after you, you were a dead man walking. After a moment the doors opened slowly. The smelled that came forth was nearly Corbin's undoing. "What wrong?" Stone asked never once looking around. "I feel something..." Loren replied. "What does this feeling feel like?" Stone inquired, inhaling loudly; rolling his head left and right, his senses flaring out.

"It feels evil," Loren smiled. Corbin flatten himself further against the wall. He'd forgot how intuitive The Triune was. They were strong separately but together they were powerful. They suddenly looked in his direction. Loren and Stone started moving toward him. "Come out. Come out where ever you are," Loren sang out. The two men were getting closer to his hiding spot.

It was Dimitri who unintentionally saved him. "Come. We must go. The NWO colony has assembled inside and is waiting for us. This meeting is going to establish true reign. The Forge has sent their Ambassadors to negotiate peacefully with us as to who should be the true rulers of The NWO," Dimitri smiled evilly.

"We should kill them before they open their mouths. They are a waste of time and space. Stupid turds the whole lot of them. How dare they even think they can even speak to us, even challenge our authority. We are legion. We are many. We are everywhere." Stone spat out.

"Calm down, Stone. This meeting is with their three officials, so we can set up our actual meetings with their actual heads in a couple of days. We want to make them think, there is hope for them." Loren warned still facing Corbin's direction.

Stone only nodded. "We must not rush things." Dimitri ever the calm one, advised them. "We've only been given a certain amount of time to do what we must. In that time, we must hit hard. The Forge is of little significance to us. We are the true leaders and we shall take our position.

The faiths of the people are at an all-time low. No one believes in their faith, family, and friends anymore. They are sheep. Walking around without visions and purpose." The three hooded men looked at each other and began laughing. Their evil sound causing Corbin to shiver. "I love it," Loren stated.

"Let's go," Dimitri led them into the building. Corbin let out the breath he wasn't aware he was holding, he slid down against the wall. "I must tell, Drakus." He took out his flask from his back pocket taking a long swig, rising he hastily began retreating. Things were about to go down...big.

* * *

Music World Gospel recording artist Amber Bullock melodic voice was captivating. It was a true instrument. She was in the middle of the song "For Every Mountain." Rayna wasn't just hearing the music or Amber's voice. She was listening to the meaning behind the words. They were essentially telling her life's testimony.

I've got so much to thank God for
So many wonderful blessings
And so many open doors
A brand new mercy
Along with each new day
That's why I praise You
And for this I give You praise

Rayna head was bowed and the tears began to flow. She thought about how a child she suffered through bouts of depression, because her father was never around to support her or her mother. Yet, she persevered, going on to college and then getting her law degree and becoming a Lawyer.

For waking me up this morning
That's why I praise You
For sending me on my way
That's why I praise You
For letting me see the sunshine
Of a brand new day
A brand new mercy
Along with each new day
That's why I praise You and for this
I give You praise.

Rayna began rocking back and forward. She couldn't help herself some warmth was resonating all over her body. To her right she could see people standing swaying back and forth their hands raised in the air. Many where saying "thank you" and Hallelujah." Rayna couldn't say anything; her words were literally stuck inside of her. She was aware how blessed she was to see the dawning of a new day and her best friend Sheila too. Sheila could have been killed by The NWO, but she wasn't. Sheila was spared. Rayna looked toward the front through tear filled eyes. Mike had his arms around Sheila; the couple was nodding their heads in agreement with the song. Now Amber Bullock was transitioning, really singing, the music went up a knot. More and more people began standing and praising and worshipping.

You're Jehovah Jhireh
That's why I praise You
You've been my Provider
That's why I praise You
So many times You've met my need
So many times You rescued me
That's why I praise You
I want to thank You for the blessing
You give to me each day
That's why I praise You
For this I give You praise.

Rayna couldn't help herself. She found herself standing swaying back and forth and crying. Just crying hard, it wasn't tears of sadness or hurt. She really couldn't explain this phenomenon. She often witness worshippers crying and lifting their hands and wondered what they were feeling. If you were to ask her, she still couldn't give an apt answer. Words couldn't describe this releasing. You just felt it and moved with it.

For every mountain You brought me over

For every trial you've seen me through
For every blessing
Hallelujah, for this I give You praise

Rayna was shocked when she felt someone wrapped their arms around her. She looked up and her heart stopped. "Eric?" He was wearing a three piece dark blue suit, making his broad shoulders prominent. Eric looked like home to her. Her safe haven. Rayna breathed his name out; she remembered earlier feeling as though someone was watching her. She knew now it had to been Eric. It's weird how subconsciously her body recognized his when in close proximity. Rayna didn't want to think about that now. She was enjoying the moment. Right now, she was happy.

Her best friend Sheila was alive. The Montgomery's, of whom she considered her second family, were all safe and happy and she was with Eric. Rayna decided to just live in the moment. She wasn't going to worry, as she knew who holds tomorrow. Eric wiped her eyes with one of the tissue a passing Usher gave him. "Are you OK?" Rayna smiling through her tears nodding her head yes and together they enjoyed the morning service.

Pops Montgomery sermon was on "Unstoppable Praise." Rayna took copious notes, she felt recharged after the service. She and Eric paid their respects to Sheila and Mike and the rest of the Montgomery clan. Eric escorted her to her car admonishing her to drive safely. Rayna smiled and stated that she would. Eric waited until she pulled off to go to his vehicle.

"You got it bad man."

Eric smiled not responding. "I never thought I'd see that look on your face, dude. Yet there it is." Bryan teased.

Eric continued to look in the direction Rayna took. He would wait an hour before calling her to see if she made it home safely. He didn't believe in talking and driving as law official he'd seen too many accidents caused by texting, talking and driving.

"What look might that be?"

"I think you know, brother. It's the look me and Mike have when our women walk into a room." Bryan stated confidently.

Eric rubbed the bridge of his nose, hiding another smile. "Was there something you wanted, Bryan?" Bryan was tempted to tease Eric a little longer. "Yes, Mom wanted me to inquire if you'd be coming to Sunday dinner with us tonight. And that should she set an extra plate?" Bryan hinted.

Eric did smile then. "Yes, I will be coming to dinner tonight. Unfortunately Rayna will not. Next time, though." He turned facing a smiling Bryan.

"I knew you were a smart man," Bryan stated.

"No doubt." Both men parted, agreeing to meet at Mom and Pops in thirty minutes. Eric mouth was watering in great anticipation, no one, could cook like Mom Montgomery. He found himself wondering if Rayna could cook as well. There was so much he wanted to get to know about her, he realized. Eric was more determined than ever to solve the mystery of his mother's death and that of the NWO. He was sure his future with Rayna depended on it.

Chapter 10

Rayna finally found a parking spot at the hospital; unfortunately, from her perspective, it was on an underground level. It occurred to her that Thursdays weren't usually this busy, as she parked and prepared herself for what would be a longer than usual trek to Phil's office.

She was conscious that she'd never liked these underground parking lots; they never seemed to have sufficient lighting or guidance signs. As she made her way towards what she assumed was the exit, wishing she'd worn flatter shoes, she tried to preoccupy herself with what Shelia had insinuated many times. Sure, why shouldn't her friend want her to find true love? There was a difference though between looking and seeming overly needy. Her casual thoughts were interrupted as she reached the exit door and heard a loud echo, somewhere off in the distance, which caused her to jump nervously.

Rayna looked around with a sense of eeriness but concluded that it could have come from anywhere. That was another thing about these places - every sound reverberated off of every surface. Stay calm; she told herself. Drawing in a deep breath, she called upon the cool determination that had helped her win many what seemingly appeared to be no win cases in the courthouse.

In the next instant, all thought of calm or collection had completely disappeared. She found herself pulled off balance and when she did manage to regain a sense of her situation, it was too late, the assailant had already struck. Someone with great physical strength had grabbed her from behind and although she had begun to struggle, she didn't think that overpowering them was a likely option. Instantly she began to formulate an escape plan and as instantly, they had their arm around her neck and were applying pressure, slowly but steadily. As she tried to struggle free, combining an awkward attempt to repeatedly elbow her attacker in the stomach, and grab their arm to stop them from choking her, she became aware of a disgusting odor.

The foul stench had her gagging. Rayna knew she had to fight for her life, that much was clear but she also had to fight back her own sense of panic. That smell - she was somewhere between heightened consciousness and delirium, what was that putrid stench?

Hit by a brainwave and feeling she was losing the battle, she forced herself to go limp in her attacker's arms. It seemed like a long wait before the pressure on her neck was eased but as it was, she caught hold of her aggressor's arm, finding and sinking her teeth into their hand. She spat out quickly the chunk of flesh and coppery saltiness of their blood seeped into her mouth. As the hold on her grew weaker, she rammed her elbow backwards hard and felt it connect with the assailant's midriff which signaled her moment to flee.

She ran, screaming as loudly as she could and calling for help at the top of her voice. She managed to find a flight of stairs, and hastily discarding her shoes, so that she could ascend as quickly as possible. All the time, as she made her way upwards, she sensed that her attacker was gaining on her, though she was unable to make him out.

Rayna was running blindly, the blood was falling fast and furiously. She relied on instinct and prayer to guide her. She had to live, this much she knew. At the top of the final flight in the parking garage, Rayna found herself falling forward, her legs having been grabbed from behind. As her head hit the concrete floor the taste sensation was akin to biting into a mound of earth and she felt nauseas. Total shock had taken over now and she could no longer scream or cry out as she was rolled roughly onto her back by the man, clothed entirely in black and wearing a balaclava.

There was nothing in his eyes, she noted, nothing discernable and suddenly, this gave her back the power to scream. In the moments of his obvious panic, that followed, she managed to successfully grab at a stray piece of glass lying close to where she'd been brought low. He regained control, holding her down while getting to his feet and slapping her hard twice, as he hauled her up roughly by her hair. Rayna could see wafts of her hair falling onto the concrete floor.

The blows stunned her; the sheer brutality of her attacker was already evident but the stringing slaps made everything seem even less real. It was like some horrible movie. She was trapped between reality and fantasy. Was this actually happening to her? Her assailant turned her around roughly, and laughed. He leaned in and to Rayna's horror began licking the blood from the side of her swollen lips.

Rayna's stomach lurched in disgust. Then she remembered the glass in her right hand and shoved it as hard as she could into the man's thigh. She took the opportunity to flee once again but within five strides her knee had given out and she was on the ground. She looked around briefly and the sight of him striding towards her made her start pulling herself forward, using her hands and arms to crawl away from him, as he gained on her.

"Come on, Rayna, move," she whispered over and over to herself. As she dragged herself along, the blood resulting from her injuries formed a trail across the ground. The pain she felt was growing stronger, but her determination to survive was an equal match for any pain. As she reached one of the parked cars, she used its bumper to pull herself up onto her feet and attempted to make her get away between the rows of parked vehicles.

At some point, her limbs were now numb, but somehow she still propelling her forward, after a while, Rayna realized that he was no longer in sight. She looked around frantically but she could no longer see him and this relief seemed to take away all her remaining strength. She lowered herself between a couple of large cars, coming to rest near the driveway in the hope of being spotted by a passer-by. It was at this point that she heard his voice; familiar, unbelievably familiar.

"Rayna? Rayna, is that you? My God! Baby, talk to me. Tell me what happened?" Eric looked down at her, concern washing over his face as he crouched to look into her bruised and swollen eyes. Rayna grabbed Eric and just clung to him crying uncontrollably. She couldn't stop shaking.

Overwhelmed with emotions, several colorful words exploded from his mouth. He drew her close to him, while drawing his Glock from its holster and surveying the area for any sign of her attacker. "Rayna stay here," he ordered. Eric couldn't believe what he was witnessing. He knew without a doubt now, that he and Rayna had some kind of connection together.

Like when he met her in the rain, after leaving his meeting with Philip; he had the strong unction to take this direction to his car. The urge was so strong he was seriously questioning his sanity. Rayna hand was bleeding profusely. Eric took a handkerchief from inside his black blazer, hastily wrapping her wounded hand. "Rayna, I need you to stay here. Don't move."

Rayna reacted like a crazy woman, "no, no Eric! Please, don't leave me. Please. What if he's still out there? Please, don't leave me." She was close to hysteria.

Eric enclosed her in his arms, "baby, I'm not going anywhere. I'm here, baby." Eric soothed. Finally, he let out a deep breath, conceding that the perp had probably fled the scene by now and that her need for security was greater at that moment, than his desire to embark on a seek-and-destroy mission.

It took no time for a medical team to arrive. He watched her being lifted on to the gurney and hooked up to an IV. All the time Rayna remained silent as she stared into the middle distance. Philip arrived moments later; he looked mortified as he took her hand and tenderly uttered soothing words of comfort. Eric stood watching as Rayna, accompanied by Philip and the medics, and was taken away, to be treated further at the Hospital. The anger inside of him had not subsided.

It felt like a tension in his upper body that needed to be released. His mind was a mixture of care and concern, fury and helplessness, and envy, as he observed the man who now occupied his space. He needed to go somewhere, to find a safe distance from others as a way of defusing the time bomb he felt himself carrying. He was a man of control and right now, he was losing that one trait that was so desperately needed.

* * *

Captain Harrison strolled through the banks of desks, sighing heavily as he came to a standstill at Eric's office door. "You know son, I am getting too old for this. It seems the world's becoming worse and worse. Monsters out there come in many forms and all races," his expression was grave, stony. "They're targeting men, women, and children. No one's exempt."

Eric motioned for Captain Harrison to enter. "We will catch these monsters, Sir. I know it'll take some time and effort, but, I have no doubt that we'll prevail." Eric vowed.

Harrison nodded, his tone becoming more procedural as he spoke again. "Now, it's my understanding that Ms. Peterson is friends with Ms. Sheila Lawson. Do you think there might be a connection between what happened and the NWO case?" Captain Harrison quizzed Eric.

Eric nodded. "My gut tells me that's the case, Sir. I'm waiting for Forensics to complete their analysis. Hopefully our assailant left enough evidence behind to make an ID for a possible arrest soon." Eric was less convinced about this than he sounded. On the inside, his focus remained on Rayna, how to protect her, and whether in her eyes, her protection actually had anything to do with him. He couldn't quite understand who'd want to harm her though he accepted that his judgment was hardly objective on the matter.

"I got another call from a journalist friend of mine yesterday. Another young female's been reported missing. One Patricia Hilliard, comes from deep pockets, her parents are piling the pressure on, up high."

Eric pinched the bridge of his nose, great, another victim to add to their growing list. "I think those NWO crazies are stepping things up, almost as if they're up against time."

"Don't get lost in this case, son. I need you to really stay focused on this one." Captain Harrison advised.

Eric became aware of the buzz that characterized the open plan office in which he worked and was suddenly reminded of the weight of his responsibility. "I understand, Sir."

"I have no doubt that you do," Captain Harrison gave him a reassuring look before returning to his office. Eric watched his Captain walk away and wondered how much longer he was willing to stay on the force, it was obviously after forty five years, the harshness of the monstrosities committed by these criminals were taking its toll of him.

He knew Captain Harrison wanted him to let go of the murder case of his mother. The twenty-three year old cold case that no one seemed interested in. Now thirty years old, Eric felt as though he was sixty, the weight of finding his mother's killer wouldn't allow him the freedom to be completely happy. Right now, he was only existing and not living. Quite frankly the only time he really felt joy was when he was with Rayna. Eric frowned.

Thinking about Rayna was causing him to grow angry again. Anger he was familiar with, but, since Rayna entered his life, it was growing into something darker. It was frightening. Eric knew deep down that it had something to do with the fear of losing her, like he almost done tonight.

Eric gaze returned to the young girl. "Wonder, what's your story, little one?" Eric studied the picture a little longer, before putting it back inside the file on top of his desk, he vowed to do some field investigation tomorrow. He returned to his attention to solving the case of the New World Order. His gut told him he was closer to solving these case than ever.

Chapter 11

Eric parked his black Yukon truck on the wide drive that led up to his spacious split-level home. Rayna sat looking less than comfortable beside him in the passenger seat. She wore a pair of his sweat pants and one of his shirts. She'd finally been allowed out of the Hospital's observation unit and he had been more than a little surprised to receive a call from her, asking whether she could stay over at his house.

Eric was secretly pleased that she had opted to call him, and not that of her best friend Sheila. The fact that she did this was testament of her, fragile state. He'd grabbed the clothes from his locker as he'd left to collect her, figuring her clothes would long since have been bagged and tagged by Forensics.

Rayna's left eye was dark, bruised and swollen shut. "I don't want to be an inconvenience to you. I can always stay at a friend's house, tonight," she whispered as he released his seat belt and looked across at her.

Eric could hear the physical pain behind her softly spoken words, "if I thought you'd be an inconvenience, you wouldn't be here. Remember, I never do anything I don't want to do, lady."

Something inside her wanted to smile at his directness but she was hurting too much for that. "I don't understand, Eric, what did he want? It doesn't seem like he was trying to, to…" Rayna couldn't even bring herself to say the awful word, rape out loud. She shivered, wrapping her arms around herself.

Eric shook his head. "I don't know, baby. Look, let's take one step at time. Let's get you settled in and we'll talk about it later."

He carefully ran the pad of his index finger over her swollen lower lip. Eric's demeanor suddenly became dark. "I will get this person. I need you to believe that, if you don't believe anything else." Eric held her stare.

Rayna shivered at the intensity conveyed by his steely expression. Yes, she believed him and she told him so.

Eric nodded forcing a smile. "Come on; let's get you settled in before Mike and Bryan arrive."

"They're coming over?" Rayna asked, in surprise. Rayna had to control her rising panic. She really couldn't face anyone other than him tonight. She looked like hell; this was why she hadn't called Sheila. Rayna knew that she would have to eventually deal with Sheila's hurt feelings later, but right now; she didn't want to see the pity in her best friend's eyes. Sheila would take one look at her and would begin crying and heaven only knows what else. She didn't want to see anyone at this precise moment, she felt dirty and violated.

"Yes, I ask them to come over." Eric reached out gently pushing a lock of hair behind her ear. Rayna held her head down as if afraid of looking him in the eyes. Eric didn't push her, but he refused to let her hide from him, to even blame herself to the travesty of what happen to her today. She was not at fault.

Rayna didn't have the strength to argue, all she wanted right now was a long hot shower and some quiet time. Eric came around to open her door, and she stepped out of the car with great care; thankful for the painkillers she'd received just before she left the Hospital. The house was surrounded by some beautiful woodland; the trees set back and generously spaced out.

The lawn was well taken care of and she was pleasantly surprised by the array of flowers that adorned its borders. Eric gestured for her to go in first and she limped passed him. Eric felt compassion for her and less than pleased with himself. He observed the lost and confused, Rayna, as she made her way up to the house. For the second time in his life he'd failed someone he cared about. Cared about? He questioned himself - surely there was more to it than that.

They arrived at his door, Eric punched in the security code and they entered; her first, him following on. Inside the large living room, she stood looking out of the expansive floor to ceiling window onto the calm waters of the lake.

"This is breath taking, Eric." Rayna said breathlessly. The view literally stole her breathe. She immediately felt like she was safe and protected. It was definitely a safe haven. Rayna began walking slowly around the spacious living room. Eric leaned silently against the door, watching his lady, holding his breath that she would be pleased. That she would be...accepting. He put his heart and soul into building this place.

It took Eric seven years to complete it. It was almost like he was a man possessed. The vision of how to build it would come to him in dreams. He would get up the early the next day and sketch out what he saw in his dreams. It was like he was building it not just for him but for someone else also. As Rayna continued to walk around his living room, he knew... Rayna was the one; he was building the house for his future with her.

"When I was a little boy, I use to sneak out late at night and go down onto the banks of the lake to fish." He was standing in the middle of the room watching her as she stood framed by the beauty of the wilderness stretching out beyond. He felt compelled to move closer to her and as he came to stand by her side, she looked into the intensity of his eyes. He held her stare and at that moment she admitted to the deeper connection she felt towards this man. It was in her heart, beating like the blood through her veins.

"I never told anyone this story; it reveals a part of me I'd never want to share publically."

She found a soothing balm in the tone of his baritone voice, and as he cupped her neck she moved closer to him.

"No one's going to hurt you now," he told her, gently massaging her neck.

She placed her arms around him and he held her close but not tight.

"I promise you, I will protect you with all my being."

She released her embrace and he released his. Rayna looked at him as though to confirm the promise in the sincere half-smiling expression on his face. She nodded and in the late blaze of light afforded by the window several moments passed.

The soft and melodic pitter-patter of raindrops seemed to bring them both back to the here and now. She was thinking about the way Eric has found her collapsed and in a heap in the pouring rain, a broad smile swept Eric's face.

"What were you just thinking about?" She asked, his smile infecting her and causing her to reciprocate.

Eric couldn't help himself, he had to touch her. It was sheer compulsion. He reached out softly ran the pad of his thumb over her lower swollen lip. "I was thinking about that day, that time when I found you flat out in the wind and rain."

Rayna tilted her head to the side and again smiled genuinely that night. "Me too," she confided. She shrugged delicately. "It seems you're always saving me in the rain."

* * *

They shared two generous portions of strawberry chocolate covered cheese cake, as Eric made preparations for the tea and she sat on a tall stool in the kitchen, the thunder's loud boom caused Rayna to almost fall from her seat three times. Rayna was quickly becoming disgusted with herself; she was like some shrinking violet. Just yesterday, no one would have ever compared her to such a thing. The rain had grown heavier now and was accompanied by the odd flash of lightening, and boom of distant thunder.

"I knew I was a recluse from an early age. I had this strange affinity to nature." Eric's voice was like melted chocolate his was rich and soothing. Rayna allowed it to seep into her. "My mind would wonder and my body would want to follow. My parents absolutely forbade me to go into the woods due to the hidden dangers but for me, it was like the call of the wild."

She listened to him intently, trying to detect what he wasn't saying as much as the words that came from his mouth. Eric's familiarity with the kitchen was obvious, he moved from point to point with an easy confidence. Filling the stainless steel kettle with water he placed it on the lit stove.

He looked around at her suddenly and found her staring keenly at him, "what's up, you prefer to keep it electric?" He smiled cheerfully.

She looked embarrassed, "not that, it's your…opting to drink chamomile tea, instead of the hard stuff. Eric's hazel eyes had turned dark, they almost looked black.

"Oh, courtesy of my dear twin sister. She continues to bring tons of it in all flavors into my home. The louder my protest, the larger my quantity of tea become, alas, I learned to just accept what I can't change." Eric shook his head. He leaned in and whispered out loud. "I will confess this only to you. I have acquired a taste for the brew." Rayna laughed. Eric found himself laughing with her. Man, it felt good to laugh freely; only thing marring the mood was the scars on Rayna's beautiful face.

Rayna must have sensed his mood, because she lowered her head again. "Well, remind me to thank her," She tried to sound upbeat but her voice was low and hoarse.

He came across to her and cut into his slice of cake, "what's it like?" Eric nodded toward her generous portion of sliced cake.

Rayna was glad for the distraction, popped another piece into her mouth, closing her eyes, letting the sounds of satisfaction that she emitted do the talking for her. When she opened her eyes again he was still watching her but she refused to be embarrassed. Eric loved that about her. He forked a huge piece of the sweet treat into his mouth and offered his own moan of appreciation. It was a moment of shared bliss.

The loud thunder caused Rayna to jump slightly and as if on cue, Eric continued his story.

"I remember one night, I was compelled and truly that was what it was, a strong compulsion. To get up and go out into the woods. I had this secret path I would take, something that only I knew about. There was nothing unusual in me sneaking out but I remember this feeling, feeling that something bad was going to happen."

The kettle whistled loudly as it reached the boil and Eric broke off to attend to it. He was back with her in moments, bearing two cups of tea and looking at her strangely. He placed the cups onto the counter and reached out to brush some of the cake crumbs from around her mouth. The movement had her holding her breath. She waited, for what, she didn't know.

Inside of her there was a quiet calm voice and it was calling out to him. His eyes twinkled with laughter and there was a five o'clock shadow gracing his face. The lightning boomed again, causing Rayna to almost jump out of her chair again. Rayna sipped from her cup of tea, hoping to calm her frayed nerves.

"I wanted to wake Erica up to join me that night but didn't. I remember climbing out of my bedroom window and running into the woods. In the dark, in the woods I felt free, uninhibited. The moon was full and it helped to light my path. I just began walking; not really knowing where I was going it was instinct really. I suddenly heard voices. Someone was arguing angrily. Hiding behind a tree; I stopped to listen and was completely shocked to recognize the voice of my mother. The other voice was of some man I didn't recognize. I heard a sound and my mother crying out. Obviously he had hit my mother. I jumped up and began running toward her. The man was too far for me to make out his appearance and he was dressed in all black.

As I was running toward my mother all I could think of was how eerily quiet the woods had become. Even the animals were quiet. I looked up and the moon was blood red. It literally froze me there on the spot." Eric looked at Rayna. "Baby, I promise you I've never seen such a phenomenon in my life." Rayna reached out to him in support; Eric immediately took her hand folding them in his. Eric was glad of the contact, as it gave him the fortitude to continue his painful story.

He never told anyone the full story of that night. Not even his beloved twin sister. "My mother must have sensed my presence because she turned in my direction and began running towards me. The man grabbed her by the arm turned her toward him and…" "Please, Eric. You don't have to continue, Eric. Another time." Rayna couldn't bear to see Eric in such pain, yet she knew he had to finish his story of that night. She leaned in closer to him and gently wiped at his tears of sorrow.

Eric's hazel eyes had turned darker. Rayna didn't think Eric was even aware of his tears. The fact that he was willing to show his vulnerability to her didn't go unnoticed. Eric had given her a gift tonight and that was his trust. She would never take this for granted.

She never thought in a million years her day would end like this. Attacked and yet she was safe in the arms of man she never thought she would be in. Eric. His name alone gave her strength and tonight or far as long as Eric would let her, she would be his pillar of strength as well.

"No, I need to finish. I need to share this with you." Rayna looked at Eric and nodded her head. She didn't want him to ever have to relive that night again. But, knew he had to release himself. "My mother was slammed against one of the huge Oak trees and the man began stabbing her. He wouldn't stop stabbing her I mean it was like he was possessed." Eric was beginning to sweat and his breathing had escalated.

Rayna got up gently holding him in her arms. Eric wrapped his arms around her, mindful of her wounds; he laid his head on her shoulder and continued. "There was so much blood, baby. Another thing I noticed was my mother never screaming. She never screamed. I didn't either." Eric looked up into Rayna's eyes. "We never screamed. "I never reached mother in time to save her." Eric laid his head back on Rayna's shoulder and continued.

"The man heard me coming and he ran into the woods. I was torn. I wanted to run after that scum bag; but as I got closer to my mother, I stopped. She reached out her hand to me. I fell on my knees beside her. I kept saying how I was sorry for not being brave enough to help her. I failed her." My mother looked me in the eyes shaking her head and literally with her last breathe she said. "Forgive."

Eric stood and Rayna gave him room. "I can never forgive that pig, baby. Never. This is one of the main reasons why I became a cop; to protect and serve and to find that pig and bring justice to my mother."

Rayna heart ached for Eric, witnessing his mother's murder at such a young age, was a heavy load to carry for all these years. Rayna tilted her head, swiping at an escaped strand of hair that had fallen over her wounded eye. "Eric, do you think that perhaps your mother was not asking you to forgive her murderer. But, was asking you to forgive yourself?" Eric turned startled eyes to Rayna.

He had never considered that possibility. He took the blame for that night. He replayed the incident in his mind a thousand times. There was so much he could have done to have changed the outcome of that night.

Certainly there were limited answers as to why his dear mother was even out there that night, and who was the man? His voice was forever in his ear. Eric was certain if he heard his voice again, he'd recognize him. The good news was there some clues left behind the crime scene that was enough to give Eric a small lead of the killer. It was small, but something, no matter how long it took, he was going to find his mother's killer.

Eric smiled at Rayna. His saving grace. "Hmm. I wouldn't doubt that, Rayna. My mother was always quick to forgive. I on the other hand am not. Not now." Eric was leaning against the kitchen counter. "I've always loved looking into your eyes," he stated, looking almost boyish in the wake of his admission. Rayna was surprised, but remained silent.

"And I always feel as though you can see me. The real me. I haven't felt this way about any other woman." Eric boldly confessed. This was it. He was finally telling Rayna how he really felt about her. Swallowing hard, Eric continued. "Rayna, I've spent my whole life trying to blend in, not wanting to be the focus of anyone's attention. I felt like I didn't deserve to be seen. To be loved."

Rayna couldn't stop the water pooling in her eyes. She refused to cry, it wasn't the time for that. Eric had just made a huge confession to her. Rayna felt lifted up by Eric's words. A few hours ago, she was falling into the pit of despair and hopelessness. Not anymore. She had someone in her corner. Someone who was once lost too, and now together, they've found each other at long last. It was the right time.

"Eric, I can see you, too. The real you." "It isn't easy to

describe the power of the emotions you evoke in me. All you'd have to do is look at me and I'd get this wave wash over me, my pulse quickens, the whole drama playing out inside my mind and body." Rayna admitted.

Eric held her gaze willing her to continue. "You're not alone, you know. I look into your eyes and I see a future with you but somehow it didn't seem as though it was meant to be. It was obvious you weren't, um, aren't interested in a future with me." She fell silent waiting. Eric had to be sure. Eric was looking down into his cup, as though for answers. Strange irony, she thought, if I hadn't been assaulted, we may not be having this conversation. The thought faded as the doorbell rang.

"Eric, I…" Rayna stared in the direction of the door. Their guests had arrived. She ducked her head, she really wasn't up for company.

Eric moved from the kitchen counter. He grasped her hand softly, "don't worry. Did I mention that my sister had a habit of leaving her girly toiletries here when she comes to stay over? I've told that girl more than once that if she didn't take that stuff out-a-here, she'd come around one day to find I'd donated the whole lot to charity. Imagine, my guys coming across that stuff in this man's cave. What would those fella's think?"

She smiled as he began to direct her towards the stairs, "through there and up the stairs, room to the left, Ma'am. I'm sure you'll find something to wear. I'm sure Erica, won't mind," he continued as she made her way slowly to the foot of the stairs. "Make yourself at home."

Rayna paused at the base of the stairs; she suddenly return to Eric slowly wrapping her arms around his neck, she did what she been wanting to do over the past year since she met Eric and that was kiss him. Eric didn't miss a beat he accepted what she was giving to him. Her heart. The rain continued its heavy descent and the thunder continued to boom. Not once did Rayna jump in fright. It was Eric who regained control of the situation. He looked deeply into her eyes. Rayna eyes never wavered she knew her heart was in her eyes.

Rayna stood there vulnerable. Waiting. Eric smiled in acceptance. No word were needed, as they allowed their hearts to speak for them. Eric cupped the side of her face, the side not bruised. He gently kissed her again, because he had to. "Go." Eric commanded. Rayna smiled saucily. She would allow him control…this time.

Rayna turned and walked up the stairs to the offered bedroom. Eric stood there a moment taking it all in. The door bell ringing again reminded him of his guests. Eric sprinted to open the door. "Finally, I was beginning to wonder if I needed to call the police," Mike groused sarcastically as he entered the hall. The three men removed their rain splattered coats and handed them to Eric.

"I am the police, remember?" Eric reminded, flashing Pops a welcoming smile.

Pops Montgomery was statuesque; a tall and impressive man with chestnut colored skin and neatly cut black grey hair. There was something upstanding and authoritative in the way he carried himself. Eric could see why church members and family respected him. Eric admired Pop's humility, above all. The older man placed his hand on Eric's shoulder and said nothing, it was all in his eyes and Eric nodded in affirmation.

"Oh, I remember alright and will never forget it. When we were ten, you reminded us you were going to join the forces. When we were eighteen, you reminded us again when you graduated from high school. You reminded us again when you graduated from college, and oh yes, again when you graduated from the police academy. Trust us, we remember Detective Miller."

Bryan was laughing as he took a seat in the Living room and

the other three men sat down.

"It's certainly has been an unusual day. I heard what had happened and came to show my support, son."

Eric could only nod, grateful that Pops was there.

"We must be thankful that it wasn't as bad as it could have been," Pops continued.

"How is she?" Bryan asked.

"She's a fighter," Eric proclaimed positively.

"Of course she is, man," Mike assured. "As unfortunate as this is, this will make her stronger. I speak from experience. Sheila comes home and relays the most horrific tales from survivors of domestic abuse. And, some of the women she works with, they've turned that pain into strength that powers their purpose in life."

"I've seen many women survive assaults as part of my job, too. This is different, though. It's just too close to home, reminder that I've failed…"

"Don't you dare say it. Don't you dare," Bryan rebuked him, "you're no more responsible for what happened to Rayna, than you are for the death of your mother."

"Bryan," Pops warned.

Bryan looked at his father, wanting to defend his outburst.

Pops shook his head, "let him finish, son." Bryan nodded in compliance.

The twins had learned to listen to their father a long time ago.

Eric glanced around the spacious room. He could still the residual of his emotional conversation with Rayna. Expelling a shaky breath Eric allowed his eyes to return to his family. "I feel like I'm freefalling. Everything is spinning out of control. I have a boat load of problems, and limited ways to fix them," Eric slammed his right fist into the palm of his left hand; the slap created was loud and crisp.

"I'm in a place of in between, remembering my mother's

murder, and am relating it, somehow, to Rayna's attack. The common denominator? No answers!" Eric stood up and spoke as he began to slowly pace the room, "I know you don't want me to blame myself, and logically I understand that as a child I couldn't have done much to save my mother that day. Just as realistically, I know I am not responsible for not being able to protect Rayna. But, what if she hadn't survived?" He suddenly stood still and looked at each of the seated men. "If she hadn't survived…"

"That is useless thinking now, bro," Bryan told him. "The reality is Rayna survived, and not only that, she's here with you. You've been given another chance. It's what you do with it now that will make the difference."

Mike was aware of how carefully they had to play this situation; Eric's temper could be explosive, especially when it came to difficulties that concerned family. The fact that he cared for Rayna was clear for them all to see. "I don't believe in happenstances.

I believe you came to Rayna's aide at the right time. If you hadn't showed up when you had, things could have played out quite differently." Mike winced as he thought about the terrible car accident that had killed his ex-wife and their unborn child; yes, if anyone knew what a loss was, he did.

Eric took a deep breath byway of containing the wayward emotions he felt, "you're right."

"Of course I am, I've always been the smarter of you two trouble makers," Mike sought to lighten the mood.

There was a pronounced silence as each man digested the significance of what had been said.

"This could be the making of our relationship, I know that much," Eric sighed. "In that respect, I can honestly see something good could come out of this."

Mike, Bryan and Pops looked at each other as though

exchanging a secret they had all just become privy to.

"Relationship?" Pops questioned, "Does she know she's now in a relationship with you? Because from my understanding, last I heard, she was seeing this Doctor?"

Eric shook his head, only now becoming aware of the significance of what he had revealed. "Man, this is so good news," Mike plugged the gap. "I can see the way Eric's been hooked by this thing, and let's face it, you couldn't have been hooked by a better woman."

"Yeah, strong and independent, a perfect match for the quiet storm," Bryan couldn't help teasing.

"Shelia's only ever had good things to say about Rayna. When I told her what had happened, she was pulling on her coat to come right over here." Mike frowned at Eric, "You owe me for that one, man. I had to deny my own wife the privilege of coming to see her best friend. And, why couldn't I tell her where Rayna is staying?"

Eric had turned serious again as he shook his head, "I am sorry I put you in that position. This is a complicated situation. Again, answers are few. Eyes and ears might be anywhere. I don't want to get Sheila any more involved than she already is. As it stands the New World Order probably already know there's some kind of connection between them."

Mike cleared his throat, "I refuse to give these monsters control over our lives. I refuse to become some paranoid fanatic watching over my shoulder every day. That's not the life I want for me and my family."

Eric nodded in Mike's direction, "I understand. A little extra precaution is what's going to be needed, until we get a handle on this NWO thing,"

"Son, do you think it's going to be a good idea for the women to attend this What-a-Lady event?"

Eric had all but forgotten about that. He weighed it up rapidly in his mind. It was very risky given the nature of the beast they were dealing with, on the other hand, there was no way the event was going to be cancelled, he was confident about that.

"Rayna's up for an award. I doubt she'll miss it. She's put her heart and soul into her community and helping women," Eric reasoned.

"I know Sheila would be up in arms about not attending. She's already purchased her dress and my tux," Mike grimaced, his dislike of tuxedos was known to them all.

"Well, Mrs. Montgomery is excited to be attending, as well. However, if it's too risky, I'm sure the ladies will understand. No awards ceremony is worth the lives of the ones we love," Pop affirmed. All three men nodded in agreement.

* * *

Once they'd left, Eric set his home security alarm and made his way up the stairs quietly. He couldn't help himself; he had to see Rayna before retiring for the night. What he really wanted to do was sit down and watch over her through the night. He knew Rayna wouldn't want that.

She would have to work the inner struggle out for herself. He would be there to support her through her journey. She would have to learn to trust him, he thought. And yes, they were officially in a relationship. He would do whatever it took to convince her that he was serious, committed and that they belonged together.

Eric eased the door part open and peered into the bedroom in which Rayna lay sleeping. His heart gave a little jolted as he stood there, pleased to see her safe and at peace.

Chapter 12

Rayna opened her eyes and was momentarily confused by her environment. Not a single area of her body was free from pain. The horror of the attack came crashing down on her, quickly followed by the miraculous nature of her survival. She felt lost, confused and afraid. That monster was still out there somewhere, what if he was waiting for her? What if he was someone she knew? As the stats stated, most victims were attacked by someone they know.

"Good morning, you're up I see."

Rayna looked up at the sound of the female's voice and stared in disbelief as she recognized the woman from the restaurant standing in the doorway. She wore a tank top vest and a pair of snug fitting jeans.

May I?" The woman made her way into the room and placed a tray holding two plates of neatly arranged food and side dishes, onto the bed.

"I made us breakfast. I absolutely love cooking in the morning; it's one of my favorite times to cook."

As the woman crossed the room, Rayna was aware of the pleasing scent of lavender before being hit by the flood of sunlight which greeted the opening of the blinds. Almost simultaneously something landed hard on the bottom of the bed and Rayna almost leaped out her skin.

"Sabastien, you naughty little fur ball. Come here."

Rayna's eyes acclimatized and she noticed the woman holding an unusual looking cat.

"Sorry, he can be overly friendly at times. But he's just adorable. I know he isn't that much to look at but what he lacks in looks, he more than makes up for with love. Isn't that right boy?" The woman stoked the cat affectionately and then placed him down onto the carpet. "I'm Erica, by the way," Erica held out her hand.

Rayna shook her hand, connecting the dots with some relief; this was Eric's sister, not his girlfriend. "Nice meeting you. I'm Rayna."

"Rayna, I hope you got a hearty appetite this morning, because, I made enough to feed three," Erica sat gingerly on the Queen Size bed and proceeded to pick up her plate. Savory eggs Benedict, French toast, breakfast casseroles - Rayna thought the food looked delicious and were truly appreciative that someone had gone to this much effort on her behalf.

Both women ate in comfortable silence, enjoying their morning meal. Sabastien, who had been siting patiently beside the bed, meowed suddenly, causing them to laugh.

"You've already been fed, so don't even try to guilt me into sharing with you," Erica addressed the animal fondly.

Sabastien meowed again, rubbing up against Erica's leg.

"OK, you little con artist. Here," Erica fed him a scrap of egg.

"So, what's his story?" Rayna asked, looking in the animal's direction.

"He was attacked by a dog, leaving his face permanently disfigured. Oh, which reminds me," Erica reached into a pocket of her jeans, took out a small bottle and proceeded to apply drops into the cat's bulging eyes. "Yeah, my dear brother, weather he likes to admit it or not, has a soft spot for stray pets it seems. Eric took in Sabastien after its owner fell sick.

His owner thankfully had a small engraved name tag put on his neck." Rayna watched in fascination as Erica placed two drops in each of Sabastien's eyes. "The problem is Eric doesn't have the time to properly take care of him, so I've taken him in. Eric can't take care of a rock bed," Erica teased affectionately. Sabastien meowed before scurrying off the bed.

Rayna noticed that striking similarity between the color of Eric and his sister's eyes.

"I heard that." Came a deep voice from the door way.

Both women looked up to see Eric standing in the doorway. Rayna was surprised by the intensity of the warm feelings that the sight of him standing there evoked in her.

"There you are. Care to join us for some breakfast? There's some toast left over," Erica cheerfully invited.

Eric shook his head. "Can't sis. I have a mountain of paperwork that needs my attention and some added business to attend to today. I just wanted to check in with you two before heading out, and to inform you that I'll be returning home late."

Erica noticed that Eric's gaze never left Rayna. "I hardly see you enough as it is, big brother. But I understand; it comes with the territory." She glanced in Rayna's direction, "I'm enjoying getting to know Rayna, and would love to get to know her more, so you do what you got to do. We're going to make it a girl's day."

Eric stepped into the room, briefly perching on the bed and casually slinging one arm around Erica. "Why isn't that a surprise? One of the many things you've mastered is shopping."

Erica laughed out loud. "Hey, you know my motto, work hard, play harder."

Rayna held her head down the whole time the siblings talked, not quite knowing how to act in front of them both. She was torn between wanting to stay there with Eric, where she felt safe, and leaving, which felt a less secure option. In the sunlight of this morning, their conversation of last night seemed like a dream. As the evening had worn on, in the comfort of his home it had seemed easy to block out the world and the harsh reality that someone attacked her. That someone wanted to kill, her? All of a sudden she felt stifled. Without warning the room began to close in on her, she couldn't breathe. One minute she was sitting in bed, the next she felt herself being lifted up. She wrapped her arms around Eric's neck.

Eric recognized the signs of a panic attack; he was familiar with them, having suffered personally as a child following the traumatic death of his mother. He carried Rayna through his bedroom and out onto the curved balcony. As he held her in the fresh morning air, overlooking the picturesque lake and woodland beyond, he tried to get her complete attention. "Rayna, I need you to do me a favor, baby. I need you to breathe for me."

Rayna was breathing heavily, she was bewildered and finding it incredibly difficult to reassert self-control.

"Look at me," Eric commanded.

Rayna seemed to respond to the command, immediately catching his gaze. In the concern of Eric's eyes, she found a soothing tenderness.

"You're having a panic attack, Rayna. I need you to relax and take deep breathes for me."

Rayna put her trust in him and her breathing began to slow.

"That's it. Good girl. You are doing fine." Eric soothed. He took Rayna's left hand and bought it his warm lips. It was just the distraction Rayna needed, her breathing was returning to normalcy.

Erica slowly approached them with a glass of water, placing it on the window ledge nearby. Eric nodded in gratitude and his sister retreated leaving them alone once more. Eric took the situation for what it was, an opportunity to hold Rayna close to his heart. Right now he was her guardian and he made a vow before God that he would protect her with every fiber of his being.

Having set her down, they sat closely on a couple of wooden veranda chairs, looking out in admiration at the majestic view. While he held her, she had cried and he'd kept her reassuringly close until no more tears flowed.

"I am sorry, Eric. I'm just disgusted with myself, turning into some kind of weeping willow. And, I'm not a weak woman by any means."

He briefly touched her cheek with his fingertips, "Rayna, I would never equate you with the word, weak. Look, the reality is you suffered a brutal attacked only yesterday. That would be enough to shake anyone up. Your body's reacting to that, that's all."

"Yeah, I am not going to be reduced to living a life of fear. I've worked too hard, and sacrificed so much. I'm not going to give all that up. I am not." She looked at him, before looking back at the lake. The waters were calm. "I'm going to take my life back."

Both of them fell silent, enjoying the tranquility.

"You should finish breakfast and make sure you take your medicine."

Rayna took this in good spirit as caring advice; she wasn't use to people giving her orders but on this occasion she guessed he only meant well.

"I mean it," he smiled. "Erica put so much care and attention into that meal; you wouldn't want to disappoint her." He felt a little guilty turning his sister's good deed to his own ends but it was all in a good cause.

Rayna sighed, "I don't want to upset Erica. I know we've just met but she seems like a lovely person." Rayna looked at him for a moment, and then they both smiled. "Okay, you win; I'll finish breakfast, and then take a shower and change."

Rayna felt slightly better after her shower. She half walked and half limped back to the bed. It was a chore selecting a couple of the things Erica had kindly left out for her to wear and dressing. Luckily, she and Erica where about the same size; the pink T-shirt and blue jeans fit her very well.

"You are looking refreshed," Erica assured as she re-entered the room.

"I'm feeling better, and sorry for the breakdown, earlier."

Erica held up her hand, "don't ever apologize for something you have no control over.

"Is Eric still here?" Rayna couldn't help but to inquire.

"No, he had to go to work. He wanted me to ask you if you would consider resting for the day, and to be sure to take your meds as scheduled."

"Thank you. I will be a good girl," Rayna joked. "I've been hustling and bustling for so long I'm not sure I know how relaxing works," she shrugged nonchalantly. "Anyways, I will sure have fun trying."

"Well that's why I'm here, my dear. I am going to help you relax. I know about the hustle and grind, seems like I've been doing it all my life. I'm not complaining because all my hard work has paid off, made me the woman I am today."

"Something else we have in common then," Rayna smiled warmly.

"Absolutely," Erica nodded. "Anyway, I'll leave you to rest, and perhaps later we can hit the online stores for a little browser shopping."

"I'd like that," Rayna agreed.

While Rayna slept, Erica thought about the positive difference this beautiful woman could make to her brother's life. She wanted her brother to find his heaven on earth. He had been through so much and deserved some true happiness. Under her breath, she said a short prayer of protection, and asked that her brother might find the answers he was looking for in the woman that now lay sleeping upstairs.

Chapter 13

"You're stifling me," Rayna hissed.

"What I am is protecting you," Eric countered.

Rayan's attention was temporarily drawn away from the rail of dresses she'd been viewing. They'd come out to a local retail park and were now standing in a fashionable clothing store surrounded by carefully displayed merchandise. The What-a-Lady event was less than a week away and she had nothing to wear. If Eric hadn't of placed her under house arrest, she would have had her dress in the closet by now.

She was still staying at Eric's place. During the first week of her recovery she has basically slept and rested. This week, Eric had been thoughtful and brought her laptop over; so that she was able to catch up on some paperwork. Eric was in constant touch; if he wasn't texting her, he was calling her on her cell phone, and if he wasn't calling or texting, he had his sister Erica do it for him. It was cute at first but now it was just plain annoying. She was very used to looking out for herself and was finding acclimatizing to these new circumstances posed a real challenge.

Thankfully, her physical recovery had been going well and her visible scars were fading. Coming to terms with the mental trauma was less straightforward. Flashbacks were still a regular occurrence, particularly during the night, and she'd come to think she would never be the same again, at least until her attacker had been caught. It was unsettling to know they were still out there, waiting. The whole thing had her on edge, and as much as she had tried to return to normal, it was just not the same.

"I get it. I do. I just don't like feeling like some helpless woman, who's afraid of her own shadow. I am not that girl."

Eric wanted to comfort her but knew she wouldn't appreciate such a public display. "The thought never occurred to me, Rayna," he stepped closer to her, smelling her perfume. "In spite of our short time together, the truth is I know you. I know you'd sacrifice your own happiness for those you love. I know that when you want something you'd stop at nothing to acquire it. And, I know that when you perceive you're too close to a situation, or someone, you tend to back away."

Eric wrapped his hands around Rayna's, "this isn't about your feeling weak, baby. Nor is it about your need to find the right dress," he moved his head, gesturing towards one of the racks of garments. "It's about you, and me. Don't run from me. For some unknown reason, God has given me you, the perfect gift, at such a crazy time. I'm not worthy of one but I'll spend the rest of my life proving to you that I can be the man you need." His stare lingered on her eyes.

Rayna felt deeply moved by his words. She was sure he could see her love for him written across her face.

"I want you to understand, Rayna. I am a difficult man and may even come across as dictatorial but I…"

"This doesn't look good."

Rayna smiled at the sound of her best friend's voice. "Trust me, it isn't as bad as it looks," she turned to hug and greet Sheila; she couldn't help but notice the clutch of shopping bags carried in by her friend. She was happy to see Mike was with her. Maybe now she could get a little shopping done.

Mike patted Eric on the back as he drifted in, "hey, little sis. I know Eric can be a little protective."

"A little?" Both women responded at the same time.

Mike and Eric looked at each other and smiled.

Where Eric was concerned Sheila was not surprised by any of

this talk. She already knew that he was incredibly disciplined and didn't share himself easily. She also knew that once he deemed you a friend or family, you were forever in his care and under his protection. Rayna watched Eric from the corner of her eye. His face gave away nothing but she knew he was upset about her and Sheila attending the What-a-Lady event. Given the circumstances, she was tempted not to attend herself but she felt she had to.

"Rayna, in the wake of what's been happening lately, it's best to err on the side of caution," Mike looked at Sheila. "I think we should all be a little more, cautious."

Sheila winked at Mike, "look, we get it. We do. It's not that we're trying to be difficult. We just don't want to give up our lives. Give those monsters power over us." She looked at Rayna.

"Looks like you've purchased the whole store," Eric directed his comment towards Sheila, trying to ease the air of tension.

Sheila held up her bags, squeaking with delight. "Decisions are the worst. I just couldn't decide on which dress to choose from, so I purchased three. One for now, and two for later."

"I am so behind, I haven't found one dress to my liking so far," Rayna groused.

"Well have no fear, my dear, your bestie is here. We are going to search high and low until your gown speaks to you," Sheila responded, leading Rayna over to another rack of gorgeous looking gowns.

Mike held up both hands, "whoa. Did I just hear correctly? Dresses speak now?" He looked at Eric who only shrugged.

"Yes they do cave man. A woman will know when it's the right fit. It speaks," Sheila mimicked her words by waving the arm of one of the more showy garments.

Both ladies laughed out loud.

"We could be some time, so you two sentinels best go and get yourselves something to eat. We'll make sure and call you when we're done," Sheila smiled at them, and exchanged a knowing look with Rayna.

Mike stepped over and pecked his wife on the cheek before picking up her shopping bags. "Sounds like a plan to me. A brother is starving."

Eric looked at Rayna long and hard before nodding and following Mike as he walked away. Rayna was aware she has been holding her breath, she reminded herself to breathe in and out. One day she was going to have to tell Eric about her not being able to have children. That was something she wasn't ready to deal with just yet. Man, life could sure throw a person a curve ball.

"I can't believe how intense you guys are, already?" Sheila gushed happily.

"I know. I can't believe it either. I'm almost afraid to believe it's real." Rayna looked as if she was about to say something more but didn't.

"What?" Sheila asked out of concern.

"I don't know. Maybe I'm being silly," Rayna paused, trying to find the words. "I'm having some doubts. I sometimes feel like I'm not enough for Eric, and that maybe one day he'll wake up and see that I'm not the woman for him. Maybe he's just feeling sorry for me."

Sheila placed one hand on her hip, "girl, now you are talking crazy. Eric doesn't strike me as a man who doesn't know what or who he wants. And from what I've been witnessing, it seems pretty clear to me that he wants you."

Rayna laughed at her friend's directness. "Sheila I am in doubt mainly because, I am afraid of how Eric is going to react to the fact that I can't have kids. Every man wants to leave a legacy behind. With me, well…" Rayna hung her head, as despair settled in.

Sheila refused to allow Rayna to feel defeated. She knew of her best friend struggle with infertility and was there to support her in every way. Sometimes tough love was needed. "It's obvious the man is in deep with you. So, my advice is to get over that false sense of insecurity your feeling, my dear, and start making plans for the future." Sheila turned facing Rayna. "Eric absolutely adores you, Rayna. That man would do whatever it takes to make you happy. You can only be honest with him, take one step at a time and leave the rest up to God. Trust me it's going to work out."

"You're right. I need to commit myself to making this relationship work. I know Eric and I belong together. I just haven't been able to shake off the feeling that something's going to go wrong somewhere…"

Sheila stomped her foot in agitation. "Stop it. Let's keep things positive, girl. Look at us, we've made it through some rough patches in our lives and survived just fine. And God has deemed it fit to send a couple of men with standards into our lives, so let's just take one step at a time." Shelia paused for effect, "and get on with finding the right dress."

Sheila smiled, nudging Rayna. "You know my motto when shopping for clothes." Rayna couldn't help but to lighten up. Sheila knew the right things to say and do. She loved her for that. "Shop. Shop until you drop." Both ladies said in unison. "Let's get to it!" Sheila led the way to the rack of luxurious clothing.

Luckily, the store was not particularly busy which afforded the women space and time to browse and discuss.

An hour or so later the women were feeling quite pleased with their efforts - having identified a couple of likely dresses for Rayna to wear to the big event. It was as they were about to go to the fitting room that Rayna had a strong sense that she was being watched. When she looked around to dispel her paranoia she suddenly found herself panicked by what she saw. Her mind raced for a recollection of the face of the man she saw staring back at her from across the store. As she confirmed the sighting, she dropped her purse - it was the large arrogant man who she'd previously seen at the restaurant.

"What's wrong?" Sheila asked in alarm.

Rayna looked down at her purse and back up to where she thought she had seen the man but he had gone. Was it her imagination? She could have sworn it was him.

"Rayna, what's going on? You're starting to scare me. I am calling Mike and Eric," Sheila was reaching for her cell phone.

Rayna grabbed her arm, "no. Don't. I just thought I saw someone I knew. It's all good. Let's just decide on one of these dresses and then get back to the boys."

Chapter 14

The clear skies, crisp breeze and mild temperatures outside made the perfect backdrop for an eagerly anticipated social occasion. Inside the venue the excitement was growing, fuelled by the attendance and antics of the local and national media, as well as the razzle-dazzle of the glamorous and celebrated guests.

Eric was both on and off duty. On this, of all occasions, he realized he should be relaxing and enjoying the evening with his good and soon to be honored lady. Yet, it was the very high profile nature of the event that had him on pins and needles.

He knew he could rely on himself, his training, to maintain a discrete level of surveillance but the scale of the event, the number of people and size of venue meant he needed backup. To that end he had persuaded three brothers – who also happened to be fellow agents, to support his efforts in ensuring things passed off safely.

"How's it going, man?" He tapped Tag's arm as he entered the main hall.

Tag was the oldest of the three members of his specially commissioned security detail.

"Waiting for the fun to begin," Tag affirmed sounding bored already. Eric wasn't fooled by his disposition. Tag was ready for the expected and unexpected.

Eric smiled, he liked Tag's style, the tall well-built man was dressed in a classy dark blue suit but you could still detect the disciplined air of an undercover officer about him.

"Only fun I want to witness tonight is up there on that stage," Eric half joked.

"Yeah, too many civilians out tonight, can't play like I want to," Laurent, the youngest of the three brothers, chipped in.

He was affectionately known as 'Onmitsu' due to his Ninjutsu martial arts training, Eric was reminded as he turned the man's reference to 'play' over in his mind. He knew that an event this large, hosting, as it did, a so many people, threw up a lot of variables – lots to pay attention to and lots that could potentially go wrong.

"Ahh, poor baby. One would think you were all played out after our last round of covert ops," Tag teased his younger brother.

"Now, that was ugly. Real ugly," Laurent affirmed.

"Don't worry, Eric," Jake, the middle brother, reassured. "We'll try to enjoy the ambience and the fine food. While staying focused on the job at hand, of course, to protect and serve, right."

Eric nodded briefly in acknowledgement as he drifted into the mingling crowd, not wanting to attract too much attention either to himself or the security measures he had put in place.

In amongst the crowd Corbin was trying to weigh up exactly what they faced. It was never going to be easy to pull what they had planned off, in such a highly populated and yet confined space. He thought about his favorite haunt, the train station; even that would have been an easier place to operate in, lots of people but much less concentration, and dozens of exits. He had a bad feeling about this night, there wasn't anything he could put his finger on but that didn't lessen his sense of foreboding.

"Can I have a drink?"

He turned to see a fine looking lady in a long flowing yellow dress standing before him and he recovered his senses, just in time.

"Of course, Ma'am," he said, politely lowering the silver tray he was carrying so that the woman could take a fluke of the carbonated juice cocktail. Tonight he was faking being a waiter, having earlier stolen an outfit from the catering supply truck that had arrived much earlier in the day.

"Thank you," the woman smiled at him.

He noticed that her smile lingered and it reminded him to smile back, "No, thank you, Ma'am." He watched as the yellow dress shimmered and was lost in the crowd. A moment later he was much more interested in what he saw; his primary target coming into view. She was seated on the Dias, closest to the podium. Rayna's creamy brown skin glowed under the fluorescent lights. Her hair was done up in an elegant bun which showcased her long slender neck.

Corbin ran through the approach he would make, in his mind, he just had to ditch the tray, and no one would notice one of the catering staff as they made their way across the room. Then as quickly as he had envisaged his next move, he was reassessing as Rayna seemed to have acknowledge someone approaching.

Corbin scanned to see who it was and noticed a tall elegantly dressed man making his way towards her through the masses. He was dressed ordinarily enough, Corbin thought, sure many men sported a tux tonight but there was something less ordinary about the man. Cop. He was a cop, Corbin thought and the increased dangers screamed at him, and caused him to break out in a sweat.

Rayna descended in order to meet Eric, reaching out to straighten an already straight tie.

"Are you enjoying yourself so far?" Eric asked cheerfully.

"I am having a blast, Eric. I truly am." Rayna looked around the congested room and took in the moves and mingles of the great and the good folk who were in attendance. She noticed Mrs. Forester accompanied, as ever, by her husband; he had invented one of the best kept secrets known to woman-kind, a sort of hybrid between the girdle and brassier, henceforth known as 'Fitted

Ones'. It was this breakthrough that had turned them into the self-made millionaires they were today, and on occasions like these, they could be counted on to attend and give generously in support of their community. Rayna loved the way the venue sparkled due to the lavish art decoration that had gone into its themed design. Large fabric posters proclaimed, 'the triumph of the survivors who had overcome the trials and tribulations of domestic abuse', and in the background the house band, were playing Destiny's Child's, 'I am a survivor'.

"I'm pleased, but I can't linger long, baby. I just wanted to check in with you," Eric backed slightly away from Rayna and looked into her joyous eyes. It was great to see how happy she looked; it made all his nervousness about her and the other guests safety worthwhile. Still, it didn't stop him from panning the room to make sure nothing was out of place.

He cleared his throat and led Rayna into the shadows. Soon, the Foresters would be starting the awards ceremony and he wouldn't be close to Rayna again for a while after that. "Rayna, I wanted to tell you, I'm so proud of you. Your accomplishments and your determination. You truly deserve your award tonight."

Rayna knew the feelings of love normally confined to her heart were visible through her eyes and at this moment she didn't care because she wanted Eric to see her love for him. So moved was she by his words and the splendor of the occasion that she had planned to confess her love for him out loud this evening.

"Laurent, everything okay?" Eric asked the solidly built smartly dressed man that suddenly approached them. Laurent was doing his bit, Eric was pleased to observe, keeping thing discrete as part of the private security detail.

"All is well on the home front. I just wanted to meet the one who's captured your attention," Laurent pointed toward the concealed ear piece that Eric had tucked inside his jacket. "I've been beeping you for the last couple of minutes, bro," Laurent said sharply, grinning like a Cheshire cat.

Eric rubbed the bridge of his nose before smiling, "you got me, man but don't worry, I'm on point, trust me." He gestured proudly to Rayna, "this is a good friend of mine. Rayna, Laurent. Laurent, meet Rayna."

Laurent extended his hand, "nice to meet you, Rayna."

"Pleased to meet you, Laurent. I do hope you're enjoying yourself?"

Laurent looked pleased with himself, "it's certainly been quite a night so far, I have to admit that. I'm enjoying the music and all the beauty this place has to offer," he winked at Eric.

Eric smiled briefly, his face becoming more serious as he spoke, "well, that's enough music and moonlight for one night, man. I think you need to be some other place right now."

"You're right, I'm needed elsewhere," Laurent responded immediately, backing away. "Pleased to meet you, Ma'am," he raised his right hand and was gone as suddenly as he had arrived.

"I am not even going to ask about him, right now," Rayna waved her hand dismissively.

"You don't ever need to ask me about him," Eric assured. "I've got to attend to something else myself, so be good up there because I'll be watching you carefully," he smiled tenderly.

"That's fine, if I feel at all threatened I'll holler," she pointed to the tiny gadget, some kind of wireless personal alarm, which he had given her earlier. Seeing that he was clearly waiting for something, she rose on her toes and placed a kiss on his warm mouth. "Now, go."

She watched him walk away; her baby definitely had swagger. She shuddered suddenly, with Eric gone, she didn't feel so confident. Unconsciously, she checked that the personal alarm was within easy reach before returning to her seat.

Corbin had managed to get so close to Rayna that he could

have reached out and touched her. He inhaled deeply, taking in her lingering essence. His cell phone vibrated. As he moved to a more secluded location to answer, he frowned in irritation, knowing exactly who the caller would be. "Yes?"

"Where are you?" Drakus was customarily direct.

Corbin looked around to ensure he was out of earshot before answering, "I am close to our target." As he spoke it occurred to him that he had not had a proper drink in some hours. "Look, I've got a bad feeling about this one."

"I don't want to hear anything about your feelings, Corbin. Just stick to the plan and everything will be alright. Do you understand me? No room for error tonight. The time of Zion is close and this girl is key to advancing the New World Order."

Corbin checked the security of his surroundings once again noticing that from where he stood he could see Rayna, who was talking with another woman. He was aware that The Forge and Zion were meeting tonight, a move he couldn't entirely comprehend.

The Forge was definitely seeking to take the lead, he thought, ever since their split with Zion their goal had been to gain the upper hand. It was all a case of egos; who was right and who was wrong. He was compelled to follow Drakus who had risen through the ranks with astonishing speed. He was authoritative, intelligent, decisive and only half as demented as the others.

"It would have been better to attend that meeting, first," Corbin spoke his thoughts. "To have known what decisions had been taken, before making this move."

"Tonight is about making our mark. Just follow the plan," Drakus disconnected the call.

"You look amazing, Maya," Rayna praised.

"Thank you. You're looking stunning yourself, lady," Maya

hugged Rayna quickly. "I wanted to thank you and Sheila once again for inviting me tonight. It is an honor to be in a room of so many victorious women," Maya's eyes looked glassy, as if she was about to cry.

Rayna reached for Maya's hands, "hey, no tears. Look around. This is a night of celebration and reward."

Maya laughed nervously, "You're right, I'm sorry. No tears. I'm so happy for you, you're so deserving of the honorary award."

"Thank you Maya. I am so excited and nervous."

"No need to be. I know you are going to do just fine. If you will excuse me, I am going to do a little mingling tonight. Who knows my Mr. Right might be in the house tonight." Maya winked and sauntered off.

From across the room, Eric caught sight of Rayna and the familiar looking, slender and attractive woman she was with. Familiar, though he couldn't recall having met her before. He was about to make his way across the room to them, when the Mistress of Ceremony took the podium. It was Rayna's turn to receive her award. Eric stood in the back watching her every move. Rayna embraced Mrs. Forester before accepting her award. Going to the podium she seemed to be looking for someone. Eric emerged slightly from his hidden place.

Rayna took a deep breath, she scanned the audience. Her eyes resting on courageous women, which she had helped in some capacity, as an officer of the court. Survivors. "I am so honored to be the recipient of this award. I am so blessed to be amongst of some of the strongest women I've ever met."

As Rayna spoke the screen behind her began to display pictures of women from all walks of life. Doctors, lawyers, mothers, sisters. All who survived that of the most horrific of struggles. Women who refused to be victims but victorious. Testimonies for women in the future. Silence was not the answer, it only handicapped future goal settings and accomplishments. Rayna learned this a long time ago. Tonight she was speaking from her heart. Loud and proud.

"I am a survivor. I have survived setbacks, rejections and disappointments. I don't want to make this a woe is me speech. I want to emphasize life is about making sound decisions and never letting go of your faith." Rayna eyes sought out Eric's, she inhaled sharply when their eyes connected. Eric looked so handsome in his standard black. His hair was freshly cut.

He was painfully handsome, no doubt. Rayna knew it went beyond Eric's good looks. It was something deeper, he was calling out to her truly she had no control over the compulsion. She had to answer. Eric nodded his head, it was barely noticeable really. But she caught it, the movement reminded her to continue her speech.

"It's also about appreciating the ones you love. Those who are there for you during the good and bad times. Believe me when I say that no one can make it alone. It takes help. Thank you to the What-a-Lady committee for recognizing our efforts to help empower women from all walks of life.

Thank you to Mr. and Mrs. Forester for putting this awesome event together. It was much needed." Rayna looked again in Eric's direction. "I would also like to say a very thank you to someone who have been a pillar of strength for me. Reminding me that I am stronger than what I think. They know who they are." Rayna nodded then returning to her assigned seat, encouraged by the laud applause.

Chapter 15

Philip couldn't quite figure out why he felt restless. Perhaps it was the sense of guilt at not having attended the charity event in support of Rayna but he just wasn't ready to see her and her new man together. So instead he found himself sitting in the park making the most of the remainder of a rare day off of work. Removing a club sandwich from his bag, Philip saluted the setting sun, "here's to another ordinary day."

"Sorry?"

A woman who had been passing and whom he hadn't noticed until that moment, had stopped yards from him and was now wondering if she was the intended recipient of his throw away remark. In the red-orange rays of the retiring sun he tried to make her out. He was intrigued as much by what she was wearing as by the fact that she had taken the time to stop.

"Oh, I was just…just talking to myself," he confessed.

"Oh," she hesitated before moving a little closer. "I thought you were…never mind, I do that all the time," she shrugged and smiled.

He could see her more clearly now, she wore a dark colored Fedora hat, a black T-shirt - he couldn't make out the slogan - skinny jeans, and combat boots. She was very attractive and he warmed to her immediately.

"Yeah, me too," he confided with a broad smile. "It was the sun actually."

"The sun?" She questioned.

"Yeah, the sun, I was just bidding the sun…fair well," as the words came out of his mouth he was already regretting them.

"Oh," she nodded slowly, as if trying to assess his state of mind.

"Don't worry," he assured. "I am perfectly sane. It was just as I sat here and watched that beautiful setting sun, I just felt like saying fair well."

"Okay."

He was pleased that she seemed contented with his explanation but he had to say something more as she was clearly ready to get on her way now. "The slogan," he blurted looking down at her T-shirt.

"Slogan? Oh, yes," she smiled. "It's just one of those things, isn't it," she explained. "You buy a T-shirt one day with that particular sentiment in mind, and then time passes and you don't necessarily have the sentiment but you still have the T-shirt."

He sat up straight, nodding, "absolutely, I sure know that feeling. 'She's got it'," he pronounced the words adorning the shirt. "Well, from where I'm sitting, if you don't mind me saying miss, you certainly do. Have…got it, I mean." He's boldness surprised him but the woman didn't seem to be unduly taken aback by his attempt at a complement.

"Well, thank you," she smiled.

"That's no problem, besides it's true and I'm feeling unusually relax. You see, at this time of the day I'm normally still be hard at work or just finishing for the day. But today, I've been fortunate enough to have a day off, so I'm feeling uncharacteristically relaxed."

"Oh, really, what do you do for a living?" She asked with sincere interest.

"I'm a doctor. A heart doctor."

Her eyes lit up and she smiled showing even white teeth. Phil couldn't move. He felt like he had just been given a reward. "Oh, wow, that's an incredibly important job, so much responsibility."

He nodded, an earnest expression on his face, "yeah, I guess it is but it's good to have a day away from the office, so to speak." As he sat looking up at her, trying to hold her interest for as long as possible, he felt as though he could stay like this, in her presence, forever.

There was something compelling about her and it wasn't just her good looks; he'd been around dozens of beautiful women, but he hadn't felt the way he did now around any of them. He stood up, "I don't mean to hold you up, it's getting darker and there are some crazies out here." The irony struck him as he he'd mouthed the words.

She held his gaze, smiling, "I wouldn't happen to be talking to one, would I?"

He let out an embarrassed chuckled, "my name's Philip, by the way, Phil, if you prefer." He stretched out his hand in greeting.

She received it and they shock hands weakly, "Erica, the names Erica Miller." Strange, she thought, how she found this man, stranger on a park bench at sunset, so incredibly handsome; his warm chocolate chip eyes, very expressive and his sweet smile, so winning. There was something beyond his physical appearance, as well, something that had kept her here talking to him.

Suddenly, he looked a little lost and she found herself wanting to comfort him. This, she knew, would be a foolish move on her part; where ever she went trouble followed. There were things she had done in the past that not even her beloved twin brother was aware of, and she intended to keep it that.

It was likely, she had resolved, that she would be alone forever and that was another reason she was so thankful to God for bringing Rayna into Eric's life. Not everyone should have to bear the burden of loneliness and he of all people deserved a decent partner. "Um, I really need to be going. My car's only a block away. Sometimes I just park it on up there, and take a stole to clear my head."

"No, it was the name, Erica Miller, is your brother…"

"Eric, his name is Eric," she filled in the gap.

"Well, that's pretty amazing, I know your brother. Well sort of, he works in the Police department, right?"

"Yes," Erica felt a sudden elation sweep over her; she was so pleased that Phil knew Eric, somehow that made everything all right after all. "Well, that's pretty amazing, I know your brother. Well sort of, he works in the Police department, right?"

"Yes," Erica felt a sudden elation sweep over her; she was so pleased that Phil knew Eric, somehow that made everything all right after all. "When we met it wasn't under the best of circumstances. Our conversation was rigid to say the least."

Erica laughed. "Eric can be tons of fun when he warms up to you." Philip looked doubtful. "I will just have to take your word for it." He stated. Erica glanced at her watch. "I am sorry. I truly must be going. It really is growing late. It was a pleasure to meet you." "The pleasure is mine. Who knows we may run into each other again." Erica waved goodbye.

Philip was going to make sure of it. His mind returned to Rayna. He knew deep down that Rayna was never really into him. She was always elusive with him. Philip wanted a woman who he could get lost in and she in him, sure they had great conversation and share interest at the end of the day there was something missing. Maybe Erica was the one because he certainly was feeling some kind away. His hands were beginning to burn.

Rubbing them on the side his pants, Phil knew his quiet plans for the evening had come to an end. He was returning to the hospital someone was in great need; as if to confirm it; his cell shrilled. "Dr. Stephens," Phil answered. "Yes, I am on the way." Phil looked up at the sky once again the yoke of his responsibility felt; he sent up a quick prayer of guidance.

Chapter 16

At the What-a-Lady event venue, awards and acceptance speeches having finished, space had been made so that the center of the main hall could become a dance floor. Rayna was enjoying the after party feel of it all, as she strutted her stuff with a less confident dancing companion; James was one of the Partners at her law firm.

Eric looked on, less concerned about Rayna's involvement with another man - he knew it was all in good spirits - than he continued to be about her and the other guest's security.

"If you get any more serious, man, you're going to start scaring the guests," a relaxed looking Mike came over to him.

"Don't worry about me, isn't there something productive you could be doing, like dancing with your wife?"

Mike looked un-phased, "Trust me, my wife and I have danced our fill tonight. I was just thinking, perhaps we can breathe more easily, now that the night is almost over."

"You know me, I always expect the unexpected," Eric visibly scanning the crowd as he replied. "She did great tonight, though, don't you think?"

"That acceptance speech of hers was spectacular. I'm sure she made you very proud. Not to mention her special shout out to someone very special," Mike teased.

"I was surprised and…pleased. Thinking of taking her out to dinner to celebrate properly, just me and her, you know," Eric confided.

Mike nodded his head approvingly, "I really like Rayna. You two are meant to be together." Mike gave him a hard playful stare, "so don't go doing anything stupid."

"Who me? No, really, I appreciate your vote of confidence."

"Confidence in you two as a couple, remember that. Because, I know you, the more things seem out of your control, the more you try to control them. And, Rayna isn't the type you control.

"Trust me, Mike. You're not telling me anything I don't already know. Something is different this time, I can feel the change. I see things differently when I am with her. I laugh at the simplest of things, man."

Mike patted him on the shoulder, "that's called, being in love." Mike gave Eric a knowing look before walking away.

Eric watched Rayna and replayed his earlier exchange with Mike; he was a very happy man, at this moment, that girl dancing right there, without a trouble in the world had made that possible. In his momentary distraction, he was slow to detect the guy dressed in white who was approaching Rayna. A waiter, maybe? Perhaps, but something about the man's very precise movements, his determined path, suggested something abnormal to Eric.

He responded by moving calmly but with hast towards Rayna's position; his eyes tracking the approach of the target of his, as yet, unconfirmed suspicions. In his head, Eric was secretly hoping that he was overreacting but the man's pace and course did not change. With a single swift action, he inserted his ear piece and activated the mic, "we have a possible suspect, bearing down on the primary target, received?"

"Not in sight," the response came from Laurent.

"I've got him," Tag's voice picked up where his brother's had left off. "This guy's no ordinary waiter, Eric." Tag warned. "I've picked up on him a couple of times now, thought he was just a sloppy Joe but now he's a definite probable."

"I'm here," Jake reminded them. "If you need me, I'm within

sticking distance."

Eric tempered his heightened state for a moment, remembering his training, so as to prime himself for the very high stakes game he felt he was involved in right now. He paused and took in the scene. Mom and Pops Montgomery were seated. They were clearly sharing a joke with friends; nothing was out of place. Bryan was on the dance floor reliving the hay day of his High School youth, if his time warped moves were anything to go by. While Mike, where was Mike? Ah, Mike and Sheila had commandeered a corner, and were eagerly engaged in conversation, as if this was the first time they'd met. Eric had slowed everything down and done a double take in an effort to verify his growing suspicions, and the Intel he'd just received from Tag.

"I've been digging deep," Jake's voice came up again. "This guy's assignment roster does not tally with his current whereabouts, repeat; the guy shouldn't be on the dance floor right now."

For Eric, this report was like a trigger going off in his head; the closest thing you could get to a 'we're going in' call to action. He was poised to move-in rapidly.

"I'm almost on him."

Jake's voice sounded in Eric's ear and this wrong footed him for a second; no go, he told himself, at the same time picking up on Jake's position which at that precise moment was halfway between the waiter's and Rayna's positions. "That's nicely done," he informed Jake. "Just let him come to you."

Eric continued moving towards Rayna, carefully dodging passed the other guests while thinking, if he gets through Jake he'll never make it past me. Was it possible to detain the man without too much disruption to the overall scheme of things? He wasn't sure but in the back of his mind was the prospect of not upsetting

Rayna's glorious evening. Eric kept Jake center stage whilst he closed in, he had no idea what he was going to do when the waiter go to him but he had confidence in Jake's ability to handle the situation. As the waiter reached Jake's position, Eric saw him halt sharply, his got him, he thought. Then, all sense of normality was lost as the perpetrator played a panicked hand.

"Everyone, back off," the man screamed at the top of his voice. He had backed away from Jake, hooking an arm around the neck of an unsuspecting woman in a long satin gown. He had hold of the woman so that her head and pinned up hair obscure his face, and he was clearly brandishing a large knife to her throat. The woman was remarkably calm, probably in shock. This contrasted sharply with the majority of the attendees, who led by those that spooked most easily, were already heading for the exits.

Eric had stopped and was now dodging fleeing guests as they raced passed him. In the heat of the mayhem he was the cool observer. He noted that Jake was staying put and that the hired security guards were trying to ensure some order to the mass evacuation. He sighted with relief as he saw Mike and Bryan leading the rest of his family away, Rayna included. "Thank God," he whispered.

"Everyone, stay where you are," the man screamed in vain, as the people just kept going. There were of course, the odd exceptions, like the man who was standing unsteadily near the waiter and hostage. Eric figured this was her husband or partner; now don't you go making any silly moves, he willed as he started to turn his attention to the hostage taker.

"How you calling it?"

Tag's voice came up in his ear and Eric turned around to locate him; seeing first, Laurent, who was far back near the podium, and eventually Tag, who was in range and had raised his right hand in recognition.

"Let 'em go, and see," Eric spoke into his mic.

"Think you can talk him down?" Tag asked.

"Let 'em go and see," Eric repeated.

The hostage taker did not look scared. Eric noted, he stood steady and there were no jitters; his hand held the knife without shaking. Too cool, Eric thought, not good. This was indicative the perp was use to killing. The room was fast becoming a ghost town. That's good, Eric observed. He slowly stepped forward, knowing that the police units were probably already on their way. He didn't have time for protocol, right now. He wanted answers and preferably without the loss of life.

"I am Detective Eric Miller," he spoke loudly and clearly, stepping forward and coming to a halt. "You really stole the show tonight. Wanna tell me why that is?"

The man looked in his direction, seeming almost pleased to have someone to focus on. He smiled evilly. "There are a lot of things I would love to tell you, Detective, but that's not one of them. I want you to tell your man to fall back," he waved the knife blade slightly, gesturing towards where Jake was standing.

The hostage squirmed a little and let out short cry and her captor tightened his grip around her neck and repositioned the blade against her throat.

Eric nodded at Jake, who took a couple of slow deliberate steps backwards and stopped again. Eric looked at the frighten woman and was immediately reminded of the day he witnessed his mother's murder. Eric's pulse quickened and his mind opened up a time hole into which he found himself falling.

It was a fresh crisp morning. He could see his mother smiling; spinning joyously in a circle. She was so full of life. The child, the him of back then, had a smile on his face, always a smile, so happy to be with his mom on this glorious day. In the next scene, he saw the spoiler emerge from nowhere, and his mother's eyes full of fear, fear and recognition – she knew her attacker.

"Eric, where are you man? Where ever you are; we need you back here with us pronto. All of you."

Laurent's question brought him out of the past. In the distant background he could hear the sound of police sirens. He blinked a couple of times to confirm the reality of the situation before him. "No one has to get hurt here tonight. Talk to me," he urged. "Why are you doing this?"

There was the hush of the near empty hall and then the hollow laughter of the man holding the hostage. "Don't try to handle me, boy. You have no idea who or what you are dealing with," he projected his anger through his eyes, in Eric's direction. "You all are pathetic creatures." He was growing agitated now. "You think you know, but you really don't. You have bought into the great illusion but the time is approaching when your true delusion will be revealed," he was slowly retreating, pulling his victim with him as he went.

Eric mirrored the man's slow deliberate progress, matching his advance to the man's retreat, "I want to be able to help you."

"Help me?" The hostage taker spat the words out.

Eric held up both hands in a sign of surrender, "I really want to be able to help you. We can make this right."

"I've got something on our perp," Laurent informed via the ear piece. "Name's Corbin Hawkins, an Ex-Marine, went AWOL in '95. Has had more than one visit to a mental institution. Suffice it to say, we're dealing with an unpredictable."

"What we have here is the beginning of something big. We won't be stopped. Cannot be stopped," Corbin sounded triumphant despite the less than favorable circumstances.

"Please," the hostage suddenly had a voice. "Please, let me go?" Her pitiful plea falling on those assembled, as much as on her captor.

Corbin did not respond but those in attendance assumed he

wasn't about to exceed to her request. A short sharp cry emanated from her mouth and it seemed clear he'd brought the tip of the blade into contact with her flesh. All the time he continued his withdrawal from them and towards an unguarded exit.

At that moment there was the loud sound generated by two sets of doors bursting open followed by the rapid entry of four armed officers. "Everybody down, down, down."

In the immediate aftermath of this dramatic entrance, the woman screamed as she was propelled forward. Corbin dipped low and crashed through the exit door.

Eric, who had temporarily gone down on one knee but who had now found and held his Police badge aloft whilst shouting his name and rank, saw the woman stagger forward before losing her footing and landing heavily on her ground; blood staining the cream satin of her long dress. A shook wave of grief hit him hard but he hit back, throwing all he determination into the pursuit of this madman. As he crashed through the same exit door, two of the armed officers followed after him.

It was dark and he could just about make out the way ahead. As he pushed his way through the next door and caught sight of Corbin a short distance away, he felt as much as heard something, a bullet, whiz past his head. Whose side are you on exactly, the thought rushed through his mind but he noticed Corbin dip as if the bullet had found its target.

Eric was closing but Corbin was not slowing down and instead of disappearing through the exit into the parking lot, he changed course and started up a flight of stairs. As the two cops drew close to him, Eric stopped, addressing them, "he's heading on up the fire escape."

"No way out," the lead officer informed him. "That exit goes straight out onto the roof.

"Okay," Eric concurred. "Then let's go find him and bring him down."

The second officer thrust his firearm forward and into Eric's hand. Eric paused for a couple of seconds as though checking the weight of the weapon, "thanks. I'll lead."

As they reached the exit to the roof, Eric gestured that he would play the 'bait'. He tucked the gun into the waistband of his pants and pushed open the door firmly, quickly stepping out onto the asphalt surface and dimly lit roof. He affected a vulnerable tone to his voice, "hey, man. Hey, Corbin." As he mentioned the man's name he heard a rustling come from a location up ahead of him. He walked forward at an even pace.

"Yeah, that's right, I know it's you, Corbin. And, I know your pain too, man. I was in the army myself, once. Got all the glory and found a lot of the misery when I returned home, too, Corbin. Just like you." Eric could hear the man's gasps for breath now and he followed them as if they were a sure fire tracking device. "They build you up, Corbin. And they break you down, man. They..." Eric stopped talking as he rounded the corner and saw Corbin standing as still as a statue in front of him. A hasty examination revealed he had no visible weapon about his person and Eric could sense his words had established some kind of connection.

"It's over anyway," Corbin said, slowly, softly.

"Over?" Eric urged.

"Zion. Zion is upon us," Corbin confessed. He spun around quickly and within a few paces had leaped off of the roof.

Eric watched the man as at first he appeared to fly and then, as is the way with all mortal things, he fell forward. There was a second of air and then, strangely, not the dull thud of a body hitting the ground. "Build you up and bring you down," Eric whispered to himself as he walked toward the edge of the roof. Down below there were the flashing lights of the patrol cars and a critical incident vehicle but no body, no Corbin. He'd entered a state of shook, engulfed by a numbness that wasn't entirely new; that came with the job.

The cops arriving at his side looked at him questioningly.

"He's gone," Eric told them. "I had him and somehow he slipped away."

* * *

Back in the ballroom Eric was sitting with Tag, Laurent, Jake and the cop who had given him his gun. The female victim had been rushed to a nearby hospital and the Forensics team were preparing to start work.

"I'm sure I got a hit on him," the cop was saying.

"I think you got him," Eric confirmed.

"So, with that wound and that great height, how did he…"

"He had helped," Eric looked at each of them in turn. "Last thing that idiot said to me was something about Zion. Zion is upon us."

The others looked wide-eyed in disbelief.

"Yep. This is what we're up against. The whole NWO thing is what this is all about."

A red haired officer approached.

"Any news of that poor woman?" Tag asked.

"The EM was able to stabilize her, seems as though they got her to the hospital in good time."

Eric stared into the middle distance as he spoke, "all in good time."

Chapter 17

The restaurant was busier than ever but tonight the other patrons were the furthest thing from his mind. It was a special night for him and Rayna. It followed on from the events of Saturday when, on the tennis court with Mike and Bryan as witnesses, he had confessed his love for her.

The brother's amazement and surprise had thrown them into fits of hysterical laughter, and this had caused him to laugh uncontrollably. Rayna had that effect on him; around her he would laugh at the most trivial things. The world was no longer black and white, it was colorful - 'all things bright, all things beautiful'.

Rayna. Her name brought to mind so many joyous thoughts. A familiar biblical passage came into his head, 'he who finds a wife finds what is good and receives favor from the Lord'. Tonight he was going to ask her for her hand in marriage. Tonight, the ring that had marked the first day of his mother's entry into marriage, would serve as an esteemed symbol of his sincere and heartfelt feelings towards this beautiful woman.

The harrowing echoes of past events were diminishing with each passing day. Love was lifting him into a place of peace and serenity. He smiled at the abundance of food neatly set out on the thoughtfully decorated table. When he'd called Vera to tell her his plans, she had gone all out.

"Well, from that smile on your face, I would have to say you have something special planned for this evening," Vera had said looking especially pleased for him as he had arrived to take his place at the reserved table.

"And you've made a wonderful contribution. Thank you," he had told her, gesturing towards the array of carefully chosen and arranged dishes.

"I'm just happy that you've finally allowed yourself to be happy, Sir. Besides, I never did thank you and Erica for offering me the restaurant manager's post."

"It was our pleasure," he had confirmed, cheerfully.

Now seated comfortably and relaxed as he awaited Rayna's return from the restroom, he felt absolutely contented. He sipped the sparkling mineral water, adorned by ice and a slice, from his tall glass. It had been three months since that memorable and rather-not-remembered evening. Four months since Rayna's horrific attack.

He was getting closer to solving the case; he felt it. Corbin still hadn't been found but he had left behind some vital pieces of the NWO Puzzle. It was quite clear Corbin had not been the leader; he'd simply been one of the misguided followers. Eric and the team had gained confidence in their increasing understanding of the case, though deep down inside, he still felt he was missing something crucial.

Rayna looked at her reflection in one of the mirrors and smiled. All her life she had been told how beautiful she was but she had never really felt beautiful. Tonight was an exception; this evening she felt positively glowing. She beamed outwardly and was laughing inside. It was all because of Eric Miller. His love had lifted her and made her feel as if she were floating on the clouds - lifted high above past hurts and trials.

As she brushed the hair from her face she turned over Eric's words in her mind. 'I love you. I am never letting you go. You belong to me, with me.' Rayna splayed her fingers and looked down at her hand. The platinum engagement ring was simple, with subtle but exquisite engraving, and the significance of its meaning filled her with wonderment. She had now confessed to herself what she truly felt for Eric and this was a foreign experience to her. Though, as a child, she had always wanted someone to love her and with whom she might one day have a family, those childish thoughts had somehow remained just that, until now. Sheila was testament that love could find you when you least expected it.

She took one last look to satisfy herself that she was as presentable as she could be and turned to leave the restroom. As she approached the door to exit, she heard the sound of heavy footsteps approaching outside. She paused briefly; waiting for what she assumed was a man to pass by but grew slightly alarmed when the footsteps just seemed to halt right outside. Rayna responded with shear panic to the sound of knocking that followed. Three dull thuds shock the door; someone was clearly planning to enter.

Her breath caught in her throat as she backed away from the door and scanned the other stalls to check whether there was anyone else in here with her. A large hand pushed the door slightly ajar and found the switches - the lights began to go out. Eyes wide and hands shaking she struggled to open her purse and find her cell phone.

She swore softly, remembering that she had probably left it in Eric's car. Yet another light went out, one more and she would be engulfed in darkness. She was not thinking straight but she did know her options were limited.

Rayna went with her first thought, to barricade herself in a cubicle in the hope that someone would discover what was going on before he had time to reach her. Then, as she pushed open the cubical door, she changed her mind. The light from the corridor outside partially lit up the inside of the restroom as the assailant began to enter and something instinctive told her to head towards that light. She bolted towards the door as it swung open, angling her body to ensure her shoulder met with it. The force she brought to bear though not great was enough to jolt the intruder backwards.

She pressed on, as the man flailed trying to reassert dominance, and managed to trap his arm. Buoyed by success and powered by fear she pushed and pushed, in an attempt to inflict maximum damage to the man's arm. She heard him stifle a yell of pain but then the odds seemed to turn in his favor as he pushed back and she began to lose ground. In the next moment she found herself releasing the door and backing off rapidly in the wake of the man's forceful entry into the room.

"Enough of your futile games," he told her menacingly.

The door was quickly closed behind him and the room went dark. Rayna closed her eyes and Eric's beloved face came clearly to mind. How would he survive her death? No, she would not, could not die. Not like this. She took advantage of the darkness and quickly moved towards the stalls.

"I'm getting tired of these hide and seek games," the disembodied voice came out of nowhere. "In times of old, women were more submissive, quicker to surrender to authority. Sure, sometimes a little force was needed to enforce but in the end they'd always submit."

He seemed to be drawing closer, she judged, as she quietly closed the stall door, felt for, found and slipped the latch into place. She could smell a pungent odor that was not emanating from her immediate surroundings and that she recognized from the scene of her last daunting attack. It was a disgusting stench that made her skin crawl.

"Won't you be a nice little girl and submit. I promise not to hurt you too much. I can't let you go unpunished, for your blatant disobedience. There must be repercussions for disobedience."

Rayna leant heavily against the door, trying to contain the rate of her breathing and listening carefully to his movements. She noticed a small window high up above the toilet.

"You are such a beautiful and vibrant young woman. I have watched you for quite some time now. And I must confess, I love what I see…" He had stopped abruptly. "No, sorry, the restroom's shut for maintenance, there's another across the other side of the restaurant."

Someone had clearly tried to use the bathroom and he had affected the tone of a maintenance man, ushering whoever it was away.

"We cannot be disturbed, my dear. Allow me to introduce myself," his voice returning to its deep chilling tones. "After we have spent time together, you will grow to accept me and the responsibilities that will fall to you. I am known as Drakus, leader of the New World Order. And, you are the chosen one. Chosen to resurrect our dying vision."

Rayna took a deep breath; the man's words were serving to fuel her despair. She thought of Eric and how much he meant to her. His face came to mind once more and she was strengthened in her resolve to be with him again, to see him once more. She calmed her nerves, moved away from the door and used the toilet pan as a step to reach the window.

"It is all falling into play now. I've worked so hard. I will eradicate the weak and establish the strong. So many will be lost men, women, and children but it will be for a greater cause."

He was surely very close now and she stretched, fumbling with the window's latch. She tried and retried, eventually managing to unlock it, the window opening as she pushed. She was momentarily stunned as she heard the man's hollow laughter which sent shivers down her spine.

"But first the King needs his Queen, together we shall create and unite dynasty."

She was shaking badly but had managed to get her hands into

a position from which she could heave herself upwards. As she jumped, hoisting herself up with her arms, there was a splintering of wood as he came through the door. She felt herself reeling backwards as her legs were dragged away. She tried to brace herself for the fall but couldn't; hitting her head hard on the toilet basin as she came down.

She felt a sudden tasted of blood in her mouth and felt a sharp stinging sensation, which she assumed was coming from a cut to her forehead. He was still dragging her and she kicked out wildly, sensing her chance as she shook herself free. She crawled to her feet and managed to avoid his awkward attempt to grab at her. The darkness was still dominant but she could make out his silhouette as she backed away towards the exit.

"I'm going to enjoy disciplining you."

Drakus began to advance on her slowly and in a split second she had lashed out viciously with her right foot, striking a low blow. He grunted and bent forward at the waist. She was bolstered by the strike and then terrified again by his instant recovery. He began advancing towards her once more.

She was close enough now and leapt at the door, pulling it inwards and escaping with speed from the room. She went left against her better judgment and as she reached the end of the empty corridor and found that the fire exit door wouldn't release, she swung around regretfully to find Drakus bearing down on her.

"This will not be another failed attempt, my dear."

Seeing him in the light induced greater fear, he was tall, dressed in black, his piercing eyes visible through the slits in the tight fitting balaclava that he wore. He looked strong and unstoppable as he closed in, narrowing down her means of evasion.

"You will learn the ways, little one."

Rayna was paralyzed; she had run out of options other than to stall him. "I don't understand?" she used all her mental energy to stare him in the eyes as though she was genuinely interested. "Why have you chosen me? Why am I to be your, Queen? I don't understand?"

Drakus was standing right in front of her now, his eyes staring into hers. She was holding his gaze in spite of the awfulness of the smell that was seeping from him, assaulting her nostrils.

"The Order has struggled for decades to find uninfected mates worthy of the great leader. Disease and deformity have weakened our world. We need a leader, a means of fulfilling the legacy."

"And that leader is you?"

Drakus straightened up as if with pride, "that leader...is...me..."

"You, the leader of the world," she said slowly, as if with great reverence. "How is that possible? Every country already has their own leader. How can you hope to sweep that all away to reign supreme?" She was concentrating so hard, knowing the only thing that stood between her and death were her words.

"You will never voice aloud your doubts to me again, breeder," he placed one hand up to her throat and his grip settled around her neck.

Chapter 18

Eric glanced at his watch again. Their food was getting cold. He would give Rayna five more minutes, and then he was going to go looking for her. His stomach growled and he remembered the event. That night he hadn't eaten all day. He was totally focused on protecting Rayna, his family and the other guests. Eric vowed he would never forget how radiant she was that night. Mike had since reminded him of the speech Rayna had given, describing it as humble, inspiring and motivating.

The intensity of her presence on that stage had convinced him that she was all-the-woman-he-needed in his life. Other memories were resurfacing too; Rayna so happy and carefree on the dance floor, Mike and Sheila's little High School style love-in, and that woman. She had seemed so familiar, standing there talking to Rayna. What was it about her? Who was she? Finally the truth hit him. He'd been investigating a high profile case involving the daughter of a prominent couple as a favor for Captain Harrison, and he'd come across several pictures of the girl.

Maya, as Rayna had later referred to her, was Patricia Hilliard; the missing daughter of Alicia and Montgomery Hilliard. It suddenly occurred that he'd seen Corbin talking to Maya that night. He stood up immediately, running towards the ladies restroom. Something was not right. "Please God, don't let anything be wrong," Eric silently prayed whilst hoping his instincts were about to fail him for once. As he moved, he removed his cell phone and hit the autodial for the Police department, it was better to be wrong loud than right and quiet.

* * *

Philip entered the patient's room, nodding to the security guard in passing. He was glad of the 24 hour physical presence but equally, saw himself as offering a kind of protection; a life preserver. He cast a cursory glance at the kit hooked up and performing tirelessly to keep her alive. He had never quite taken the flashing, bleeping, respiring gadgetry in his stride. For him, the equipment was a reminder that the patient was dependent and all his effort as a medical practitioner went into retaining people's independence.

She was lying flat in the bed, her head propped up on a thin pillow. Both of her hands rested atop the covers which had been folded over just above her waist. He checked her vitals and was satisfied with her progress. Her body was recovering from the trauma it had endured and he felt it was just a matter of time before she emerged from the coma.

He was about to walk out when he thought he detected a slight movement of the little finger on her right hand. He stood still and watched intently, praying that she would move her finger again. Suddenly his hands began to burn hot.

He glanced at the water pitcher on the bedside table and for a moment was tempted to dip his hands into the cool water but he knew that wouldn't help. He had to touch something, someone. Philip approached the head of the bed and slowly reached out. Placing two fingers of each hand on her temples he began to rub gently.

"Come on, little one. Do it for me one more time," softly, he spoke the words of his will. Nothing, he concluded after two or three minutes. He sat down in the bedside chair and sandwiched her cool hands in his warm ones. "I think it's time now to come back to the land of the living, sleeping beauty. There are so many people who are waiting to meet you…to talk to you. And I'm one of them. I think you're an amazing young woman," he whispered, leaning in close to her ear; he could feel something, the slightest movement of her fingers.

* * *

Victoria felt as though she was being pulled in two directions. She could hear a man's voice begging her to return. Return to where? At the same time she could hear the sound of a woman crying. It was all very confusing. Victoria looked ahead of her, a long passageway bathed in intense white stretched out in front. She began walking in the direction she thought the woman's cries were coming from. When she heard the man's voice again, gentle, soothing, she stopped and looked back. Where she'd come from and where she was headed looked the same; how could she decide which way to go?

The man was calling out to her, telling her to come home. What was right? What should she do? The anguish that she detected in the woman's cries was obvious, immediate. She stood there and listened and didn't know what to do. She held her head in her hands and screamed for it all to stop.

When she opened her eyes she could she a man violently shaking a woman who looked as though she was on the verge of passing out. Victoria stretched out her hand as if to intervene but her gesture had no impact; what she was seeing was real but she was a viewer and not a participant. Victoria cried out, "You must survive. You will not die." The victim's eyes seemed to widen in recognition, she had cleared received the message.

The vision blurred and then sharpened. This time she could see a tall man dressed in a suit hammering on the door before entering a ladies restroom. He was franticly looking for something, someone. He looked agitated as he studied the room for clues and Victoria knew he was looking for the distraught woman.

"Hurry, please. You must help her," she willed the man and then she felt herself being pulled backwards. She tried to stand her ground but the force exerted on her was too great and she found herself stepping backwards against her wishes. It was the man's voice that was winning out. It was telling her to come home, that she was needed and that felt so good.

After walking alone for so long, those comforting words sounded like the sweetest music. The visions were fading as the man's voice grew louder but she could just make out the woman once again. In this, her last attempt, she would pour all of herself into making a difference. "You will not die this night. Do you hear me? Like me, you too are needed. Do what you must, to survive. Help is on the way."

Victoria felt as though she was freefalling, rushing backwards as if sucked into a powerful vortex. She held out her hands trying to find something to hold onto but there was nothing.

Philip was squeezing the girl's hands in hope. Her eyes were fluttering rapidly. He examined her eyes with his ophthalmoscope and concluded that she was definitely regaining consciousness. "Come on," he spurred her on. "Come home, baby girl. Fight to live. I know you're tired but push through this for me," he coaxed.

Victoria could see images passing as she fell. She saw her mother holding her as a baby; she saw her grandmother seated, with her at her side. She saw herself as a teenager and she knew the picture had been captured on the day that her grandmother had died. The images where emerging and then streaming passed, making her cry. She didn't have much further to fall and she felt the ground rushing up to meet her. In the seconds that were left, she saw the man and woman that she had tried to help, clinging together and then torn apart. She willed them to persevere, to re-find one another. She wanted to call out words of encouragement to them but she couldn't. The image faded and everything went dark.

Philip was smiling in amazement and disbelief as she opened her eyes. He held onto one of her hands and raised the head of the bed to make her more comfortable before pushing the 'call' button. "You did it, little one. You came back."

Victoria's mouth felt dry and she struggled to swallow. She wanted to speak but was unable.

Philip poured a glass of water from the pink bedside pitcher and held it against the woman's lips.

After sipping the water, Victoria studied Philip closely before asking, "Where am I?"

"You're at the hospital. You've been with us for a while now but don't you worry about a thing. It's just so great to have you back...with us." He urged her to sip a little more water before placing the glass back on the bedside table. "Now tell me, do you have a name?"

"My name is Victoria. Victoria Lawson."

Philip hid the shock he felt, looking at the girl a new in the light of what she had just told him. Erica had mentioned that she knows a Sheila Lawson, some relation to the family - could this girl also be related?

Chapter 19

Rayna sat awkwardly in a cramped space in the back of a large truck. It was dimly lit, cluttered with a variety of artefacts and smelt like a sewer. Having half throttled her in the empty corridor of the restaurant, Drakus had convinced her to comply and she'd been marched across the large parking lot and bundled into to the black truck. Her hands and ankles were bound with tape. He sat in front of her touching her cheek with his foul smelling fingers and looking at her face closely.

"Already the movement has begun. We are legion, a powerful sect and we will soon take our rightful place at the helm of this world."

She was tilting her face away from his touch but she was still very much aware that she needed to keep him engaged, so as to stall for time.

"Think little one, how do you suppose I am able to find you and the others with such ease?"

She raised her eye brows to indicate that she didn't know.

"I have eyes and ears everywhere. So you see, it is impossible for you to escape for long. You might think that you can evade me but I'm always watching, waiting."

She was about to fain interest by asking another question when the vehicle's rear doors suddenly opened. Rayna's heart slammed against her chest as a woman entered, followed by a man. How could she warn the woman that she was in danger? The doors slammed shut behind the newcomers.

"I see you two were finally able to make it to the party," Drakus quipped flatly.

"We thought we spotted some unnecessary activity in the lot but it was just some stupid kids showing off their stupid cars," the man spoke.

"You're not going to hurt her are you?" The woman asked softly.

Rayna could see her face now and the realization that it was someone she'd taken to be her friend made her feel sick.

"What I do with her is none of your concern, breeder. Just follow and obey orders, like you were born to do."

"Keep out of this, Patricia," the man warned her.

Patricia. That's Maya, Rayna almost said. As it began to sink in, Rayna did a double take, questioning the very basis of her grip on reality.

Drakus had clearly picked up on her thoughts, "that's right. This is Patricia, not Maya. Soon you will understand the lies and deception that has been taking place for years. This country, like all the others, is falling apart because of weak leadership and a preoccupation with the frivolous," he seemed to be enjoying the fruits of her confusion. "People are blinded to the realities of what is taking place, what is right before their eyes. These insects are willingly giving themselves up, family and friends, for a materialistic lifestyle."

The man who had just entered the vehicle chuckled, something clearly tickling him. Drakus looked around sharply at him and he promptly fell silent.

"Corbin, Patricia and millions more, all see the importance of change. Some will embrace and others will hate but it matters not, we are on the rise."

"I'm beginning to see," Rayna lied. "I'm beginning to understand." She looked at the three crazies realizing that the only play left was to play for time.

"We are going to birth a new generation, Rayna. A pure breed.

We'll be treated like a Queens, respected, revered," Patricia revealed proudly.

"Like Queens?" Rayna widened her eyes convincingly.

"Yeah, imagine. Like real Queens. Needed, wanted, cherished. It's all I've ever really wanted, you know. To be loved and to start my own family. My parents couldn't care less about me; they care more about their reputation than about their own daughter. My boyfriend, well ex. He turned out to be a no good cheating fraud. He was just out for what he could get. He manipulated me, and after I'd confided all my woes."

"That's rough, I can see that," Rayna told her. "It's just such a surprise, to find out everything I thought I knew was a pack of lies."

"We never know the truth in this world," Patricia looked at her seriously. "We don't know anything but the promise lays in wait for us, Rayna. The true promise lays in wait. Our chance to be creators of life, mothers of many. To belong, to be needed."

"I can begin to see what this all means," Rayna announced, looking at each of them and slowly nodding her head.

"Enough talk," Drakus bellowed. "We have got to move now. You two get back up front; we are getting out of here."

Eric had found Rayna's purse lying at the far end of the corridor and had cautiously opened the fire exit door and made his way out into the parking lot. He scanned the lot rapidly, at first not seeing anything untoward but then noticing a large black truck parked at the far end, away from most other vehicles. His mind clicked back to the view he'd had as he had peered down from the rooftop of the conference venue, on the night of the What-a-Lady event – after his failed pursuit of Corbin. He hadn't taken much notice of it at the time but it had obviously lodged in his subconscious and now the two sightings fused. He had seen this black truck before; now he had his target.

He redialed the department and apprised them of the situation, the last thing he needed was a hoard of flashing lights and sirens throwing the whole joint into turmoil. He moved swiftly, closing in on the truck so as to ensure he couldn't be spotted by its inhabitants. As he reached it, the rear doors began to open and he ducked around the side, listening intently. He could make out one man's voice but it was clear he was talking to someone else.

"...stick to the plan."

At the rear of the truck, someone stepped out and they were quickly followed by another. Eric dropped to the ground and rolled out of sight under the vehicle. He watched the feet of the two suspects, carefully determining that he was dealing with a male and female based on their footwear. The front doors of the truck opened and slammed shut; driver-side first, and then passenger side. He moved swiftly, scooting out on the passenger-side and stepping up to the front of the vehicle.

In one smoothly coordinated movement, he wrenched the wing mirror forward, so as to be hidden from its view, and wrapped on the passenger's window before springing back out of sight. As the woman made to open her door he lunged forward, wrenching the door from her grasp and pushing it open, propelling her out of the vehicle and onto the tarmac.

She gave a startled cry and he followed up, administering a single blow across the flat of her back with his forearm and succeeding in sending her sprawling to the ground. As he leaped back out of sight, on the passenger-side he heard some noises emanating from the van, another voice, deep, male. He caught his breath and rallied as he heard what he knew was Rayna's voice, albeit muffled by the containment of the truck.

"I'm here, baby," he whispered, as though his words could reach her.

The woman lying on the ground was sobbing; unsurprisingly

she seemed startled but was just starting to push herself up off the tarmac.

"Stay down, Patricia," Eric shouted.

The driver side door opened, a man hopped out and made his way around the front of the vehicle. "This is where it ends, Eric."

Corbin was yelling as he came into view but Eric was ready for him and lashed out, striking his right knee hard with a twisting kick, forcing Corbin to cry out in pain whilst his body pitched to the right.

Corbin didn't go down but instead managed to bring his head up, slamming it into Eric's jaw. Corbin threw a short left that connected with Eric's cheek. He drew back slightly, wincing as the sharpness of the pain assaulted him; still managing to dodge Corbin's next attempt.

Eric went low, taking his weight on his left leg and repeating his first move, swinging his leg around to kick Corbin on the outside of his right knee with precision. There was the sound of bone cracking. Corbin screamed and Eric stepped back, rocking on the balls of his feet. Corbin went down onto the busted knee this time, his face looked contorted with pain but he began to laugh in a demented fashion.

As Eric reassessed the situation; he was distracted for an instant by the sound of Rayna's voice. She yelled his name defiantly from inside the black truck. His pulse quickened and he had to stifle the rage that welled up from the pit of his stomach. The blood stains in the restroom that he had conveniently managed to shove to the back of his mind, came to the forefront. Had they hurt her? How badly had they hurt her?

"You think you've won? Think again!" the words spat out.

As he looked back to Corbin, he saw that the man was brandishing a hunting knife and as his words cried out, had launched himself forward. Eric brought his hands together, palms first, to clap Corbin's wrist hard, as the blade came towards him. The man groaned, as much from the pain of the effort it now took to move on his busted knee, as from the blow he'd sustained. The knife flew from his hand and clattered over yonder, while Eric brought a crunching elbow into contact with Corbin's neck. The man's head made a hollow metallic thud as it hit the side of the truck and Corbin fell forward; unconscious Eric attested.

Eric was breathing heavily but he knew his work was far from done. Out on the main street he noticed the patrol cars were approaching but he knew he couldn't wait for reinforcements whilst Rayna's life was still in danger.

"Corbin? Corbin?"

He heard the deep tones of the male voice emanating from the truck again. It was time to go in, he decided. Eric spun around and moved towards the rear of the truck but before he had reached the doors, they sprang open wildly. He dodged backwards and swerved to avoid them, only to see Rayna shoved out of the back of the vehicle. Her feet hit the ground first but the momentum carried her forward.

Led purely by instinct, Eric was in position within a split second to cushion her fall. His eyes darted over the cut and bruised face of his baby and he felt an uncontrollable up swell of guilt and remorse. She looked up at him, the shock on her face becoming relief. He cradled her, as if trying to convey his love in waves, transmitted by his heart through the arms and hands with which he held her.

A figure dressed entirely in black leaped from the back of the truck. Eric looked up, catching the ferocity in the man's hateful eyes but before he could react, the man was fleeing the scene at speed. Two patrol cars swizzed into position. Six officers sprang out; two taking up pursuit of the black clad runner, whilst two attended to Patricia and one cast a cautious eye over the motionless body of Corbin.

"Detective Miller? Are you alright, Sir?" One of the police officers rushed over to Eric and Rayna.

Eric eased Rayna down carefully and used the knife discarded by Corbin to cut the tape binding her ankles and wrists. Her gaze did not leave him.

"We are fine, officer," Eric confirmed. "We're gonna need a paramedic unit and some forensics down here a-sap."

Rayna rubbed her wrists before throwing her arms around him, he hugged her tenderly.

"Yes, Sir, we're on it. I already radioed in for an ambulance," the officer proceeded to assist his colleagues.

Rayna released Eric and gently touched his face. The tears began to flow.

"I thought I wasn't going to live to see your beautiful face again. That I wouldn't get a chance to see our love grow and flourish, Eric."

Rayna began to cry hard and he felt her pain and the strength of his own feelings towards her deep in his chest. He had no words, the only thing he could do was hold her tight; their immediate vicinity rapidly undergoing change, to become a crime scene.

Having managed to evade the cops who had tried to pursue him, Drakus watched from the shadows. The dark path to the new world was not without its infuriating obstacles, he reflected bitterly. He wouldn't give up, he had another plan. Zion will rise. Spitting on the ground, he turned to become one with the night.

***

Mike and Sheila formed an emotional welcoming party when Eric and Rayna arrived at Eric's home. Earlier Eric had called his sister Erica and the Montgomery's, briefly filling them on what had happen that night. Of course, Sheila would be here waiting or her best friend's return. Rayna was barely out of the car when

Sheila rushed forward to embrace her; the two women clung to one another. Mike and Eric's hug was far more restrained.

The two couples sat in the comforting surroundings of the living room and turned over events. The women shared their hearts and the men shared the implications of what had happened. They were both fiercely protective of their women and this was a reminder of the practical limitations of that ability to protect. Respectively, they both knew that Rayna and Sheila prized their independence. The extraordinary nature of recent occurrences was unlikely to temper the women's views on the subject of their autonomy, once the dust had settled. In relief and gratitude, the four talked collectively and individually into the early hours of the morning; it was like therapy, a way of comprehending the drama that had entered Rayna and Eric's lives.

Later, the couples sat quietly enjoying each other's company.

"I've learned never to take life for granted." Rayna lay in Eric's arms.

He held her securely, "that's a great lesson, baby. And, I was thinking, we shouldn't wait unnecessarily, but should let our feelings out as soon as we feel them."

The pleasant surprise was clear for Mike and Sheila to see written across Rayna's face, was this Eric talking.

Eric cleared his throat. "So, I'd like to ask you to marry me, to become Mrs. Eric Miller? That is, if you will still have me?"

Mike and Sheila looked at each other with huge smiles on their faces.

"Rayna, I know the decision is all yours, I don't want to influence you at all…" Mike spoke up.

"Yes we do, Rayna. We want to influence you, big. We can all see the love you both have for each other. And like you stated, life shouldn't be taken for granted," Sheila encouraged.

Mike pulled his wife into his arms, "I couldn't have said it any better, Sheila. Life isn't in the material, although that contributes. Life is to be shared, and particularly to be shared with the ones, special one you love," he looked deeply into his wife's eyes.

Eric and Rayna exchanged knowing looks as their friends talked. Rayna held Eric's face softly between her hands. Eric's eyes were watering, a tear had escaped. That spoke volumes to her. He was strong and honorable, he was gentle and caring. Eric was her home, her safety net - everything she wanted and needed.

"I know you think that you've failed me, Eric, but you haven't. Quite the contrary, you've inspired me to live, to tap into my inner self and be the real woman. I was frightened of the unknown, and I tried to compensate by trying to protect and help others," Rayna began crying.

Eric remained still, knowing she had to continue to free herself in order for them to move on.

"All the time I was praying to God. Please send someone to love me, too. Someone I can give 100 percent of my love to, and who can reciprocate. God has heard me. You're my guardian." she paused to wipe the tears from her cheeks. "I know there will be rocky roads, tumultuous challenges, but I'm up to the challenge."

Eric took her hands into his. "I'm one blessed man. I don't know why I was chosen for you. But, I'm glad. I was down in the lowest of pits, baby. Then, I found you in the midst of my storm."

Rayna smiled, remembering their first meeting, in the wind and the rain.

"Your love lifted me out of despair and tomorrow will not be soon enough for me to make you my wife. I've already spoken with Mom and Pops about it. Rayna I know you're my promised woman from God." Eric rummage in the pocket of his pants and pulled out a small decorative black box. He fumbled briefly but opened it to reveal his mother's 18 karate, chocolate and white diamond crossover wedding ring.

Rayna's eyes widened with surprise.

"Breathe for me, baby. Breathe. I need you to collect your thoughts so that you can answer my question. Would you do me the honor of carrying my name, becoming the mother of my children? Working with me to building a legacy?"

Rayna wrestled the overwhelming emotions she felt, breathing in deeply and out, in multiple short bursts, in order to calm herself. Rayna stood there barely able to breathe. She knew she had to tell Eric of her not being able to physically have kids.

"Baby?" Eric took both of her hands in his, Rayna wanted to pull away, but Eric wouldn't let her. Sheila looked at Mike tears swelling up in her eyes. Mike stood gently pulling Sheila up. "We are going to give you guys some privacy." Rayna spoke finally. "No, pleased don't leave. Sheila and Mike you already know of my... issue. I refuse to be held captive any longer."

She looked at Eric. "Years ago, I was diagnosed with a female health issue. Endometriosis." Eric eyes widened with fear. Rayna squeezed Eric's hand in comfort. "I am alright, babe. Unlike some of other women suffering from Endometriosis, I was fortunate that subjective treatment worked. But, it caused me not to be able to have children." Rayna pulled her hand out of Eric's, crossing over to the other side of the room, she couldn't bear to see the disappointment in his beautiful eyes. Rayna stood looking out the window, her slender frame shaking. The sun was slowly rising, reminding her how blessed she was to survived the night.

Eric walked up to Rayna gently turning her to face him. She wouldn't...couldn't look at him. He gently lifted her chin, willing her to look at him. Rayna kept her eyes down cast. Eric waited. She finally looked up into his eyes. "I want you to not only hear me, but to listen to what I am saying to you, baby. I love you, Rayna. With all my heart and soul. You will be the mother of my children." Rayna shook her head, preparing to say something.

Eric place his finger on her lip, effectively silencing her. "Honey, we will have our legacy. I am a strong believer that God doesn't make mistakes. We may not start our family in the traditional sense. But, we will have our family. I promise you. Now, answer me. Will you marry me?"

Rayna couldn't stop crying. Inwardly she bravely wrestled the overwhelming emotions she felt, breathing in deeply and out, in multiple short bursts, in order to calm herself. "Eric, are you sure this is what you want?" She was scared he would say no, but, had to ask.

"I don't want any other woman and you know me, I never say anything I don't mean, sweet heart," he told her sincerely.

"Say yes, girl," Sheila yelled impatiently, making everyone laugh out loud.

Slowly Rayna reached for the small decorative box, taking it from Eric's trembling hand, "yes," she declaimed firmly.

As she held the box, Eric removed the ring from its mount and slipped it onto her finger.

"It fits perfectly - just like us," Rayna stated. Eric nodded his head in agreement. "Exactly like us, baby." Eric pulled her into his arms softly kissing her. Sheila screamed, jumped up and started shuffling around the room in an exaggerated victory dance. Mike laughed before getting up and joining her.

Rayna then Eric joined them in a joyous group hug. They may not have all the answers, their journey may be difficult but with family, friends, and faith, they knew they would make it. Behind the house the sun rose, heralding in a new day.

Epilogue

"Not quite two months have passed, since the disturbing incident that took place at The Heart and Soul Restaurant." The pretty news reporter stated mechanically. "Patricia Hilliard, daughter of the ultra-wealthy Alicia and Montgomery Hilliard, has been acquitted, following her plea of insanity, and will not be serving prison time for her involvement in the New World Order related case. We will keep you up to date as we have more information. Now back to you, John."

Victoria turned the television off. She looked around the room with a frown. Although she was healing physically, her heart was in good shape considering and she felt less tired, emotionally there was still some way to go. She was in hiding, whilst acknowledging that she couldn't hide from the world forever. Everything seemed so overwhelming, so intimidating, and admitting the real motives for her self-imposed isolation would, she felt, reveal her utter cowardice.

Often she would reflect on the vision that had occurred during her comatose state, although she wasn't sure of its meaning. Perhaps it was a premonition of what was to come. The darkness that had surrounded and isolated the couple, still made her shiver. Fate, she thought, had somehow seen fit to bring her into their circle.

After her recovery from the coma, Sheila and Rayna had visited her faithfully. At first, she had thought they were just being friendly but in truth, it ran deeper; their visits were a sign of their genuine care for her. When she finally got up the courage to ask them why they were devoting so much of their time and effort towards her, she had been taken aback by the explanation.

She and Sheila were actually siblings. They were two of their father's countless offspring, brought into the world in a misguided belief that he was creating a chosen generation; a New World Order.

Victoria could hardly comprehend what the women had told her. She had thanked them for their kindness but made her excuses, telling them she needed time to take it all in. In time she might be able to embrace these women and take on board what it was they were so convinced she should know. She wasn't a praying woman but she found herself praying. "God, if you are listening, please protect me and my friends. We all need some happiness, after all the hell we've been through."

Looking out of the window at that moment, she saw Rayna and Sheila pull up into the drive and she was filled with happiness at the prospect of seeing them again.

ABOUT THE AUTHOR

Vanessa Richardson is an author, poet, and playwright. She has written several stage productions and have been blessed to perform them at various venues. Her stage productions include: *Someone to Love Me, Why Do Bad Things Happens to Good People? Lord, I Don't Understand,* and *The Fullness Of Time.*

Vanessa wrote her freshman Nonfiction inspirational novel titled, The Certain Ones. A spiritual impacting novel that inspires her readers to know that not everyone are called into greatness. Fact: Many cannot handle the process that goes along with becoming great. Only the certain ones, who endures; can obtain destined greatness.

Vanessa also host the blogtalkradio show *The Certain Ones* airing live on Thursdays 6:00pm EST. Vanessa is also the Founder and Chief-In-Chief of The *Certain Ones Online Magazine* an inspirational online magazine highlighting authors, health, entrepreneurs, and ministries. Its central theme is to inspire the aspiring ones into their destiny! Vanessa Richardson, is an author, minister, and playwright. She utilizes **The Certain Ones Magazine** and **The Certain Ones Talk Show** to connect with like-minded people to build bridges that leads to business, spiritual, and physical success.

www.ingramcontent.com/pod-product-compliance
Lightning Source LLC
Chambersburg PA
CBHW071717140626
46557CB00012B/899